SHAKESPEARE

KING HENRY IV

PART 1

NOTES

COLES EDITORIAL BOARD

OTABIND

Bound to stay open

Publisher's Note

Otabind (Ota-bind). This book has been bound using the patented Otabind process. You can open this book at any page, gently run your finger down the spine, and the pages will lie flat.

ABOUT COLES NOTES

COLES NOTES have been an indispensible aid to students on five continents since 1948.

COLES NOTES are available for a wide range of individual literary works. Clear, concise explanations and insights are provided along with interesting interpretations and evaluations.

Proper use of COLES NOTES will allow the student to pay greater attention to lectures and spend less time taking notes. This will result in a broader understanding of the work being studied and will free the student for increased participation in discussions.

COLES NOTES are an invaluable aid for review and exam preparation as well as an invitation to explore different interpretive paths.

COLES NOTES are written by experts in their fields. It should be noted that any literary judgement expressed herein is just that – the judgement of one school of thought. Interpretations that diverge from, or totally disagree with any criticism may be equally valid.

COLES NOTES are designed to supplement the text and are not intended as a substitute for reading the text itself. Use of the NOTES will serve not only to clarify the work being studied, but should enhance the readers enjoyment of the topic.

ISBN 0-7740-3201-4

COLES PUBLISHING COMPANY
TORONTO - CANADA
PRINTED IN CANADA

Manufactured by Webcom Limited
Cover finish: Webcom's Exclusive **DURACOAT**

CONTENTS

WILLIAM SHAKESPEARE
LIFE AND WORKS
Biographical Sketch

With the epithet "Dear Son of Memory", Milton praised Shakespeare as one constantly in our memories and brother of the Muses. Certainly no other author has held such sway over the literary world, undiminished through some three and a half centuries of shifting artistic tastes. Shakespeare's plots and his characters have continued to be a living reality for us; as his well known contemporary Ben Jonson wrote, in a familiar tribute, "Thou . . . art alive still, while thy Booke doth live,/ And we have wits to read, and praise to give."

The Early Years

Despite such acclaim and the scholarship it has spawned, our knowledge of Shakespeare's life is sketchy, filled with more questions than answers, even after we prune away the misinformation accumulated over the years. He was baptized on April 26, 1564, in Holy Trinity Church, Stratford-on-Avon. As it was customary to baptize children a few days after birth, we conjecture that he was born on April 23. The monument erected in Stratford states that he died on April 23, 1616, in his fifty-third year.

William was the third child of John Shakespeare, who came to Stratford from Snitterfield before 1532 as a "whyttawer" (tanner) and glover, and Mary Arden, daughter of a wealthy "gentleman of worship" from Wilmecote. They married around 1557. Since John Shakespeare owned one house on Greenhill Street and two on Henley Street, we cannot be certain where William was born, though the Henley Street shrine draws many tourists each year. William's two older sisters died in infancy, but three brothers and two other sisters survived at least into childhood.

Shakespeare's father was fairly well-to-do, dealing in farm products and wool, and owning considerable property in Stratford. After holding a series of minor municipal offices he was elected alderman in 1565, high bailiff (roughly similar to the mayor of today) in 1568, and chief alderman in 1571. There are no records of young Will Shakespeare's education (though there are many unfounded legends), but he undoubtedly attended the town school maintained by the burgesses, which prepared its students for the universities. Ben Jonson's line about Shakespeare's having "small *Latine*, and lesse *Greeke*" refers not to his education but to his lack of indebtedness to the classical writers and dramatists.

On November 27, 1582, a licence to marry was issued to "Willelmum Shaxpere *et* Annam Whateley *de* Temple Grafton," and on the next day a marriage bond for "Willm Shagspere" and "Anne Hathwey of Stratford" was signed by Fulk Sandells and John Richardson, farmers of Stratford. This bond stated that there was no "lawful let or impediment by reason of any precontract, consanguinity, affinity, or by any other lawful means whatsoever"; thus "William and Anne (were) to be married together with once asking of the banns of matrimony." The problem of Anne Whateley has led many researchers and some detractors to argue all kinds of improbabilities, such as the existence of two different Shakespeares and the forging of documents to conceal Shakespeare's true identity. The actual explanation seems to be simple: the clerk who made the marriage licence entry apparently copied the name "Whateley" from a preceding entry, as a glance at the full sheet suggests. (Incidentally, Nicholas Rowe in his life of Shakespeare, published in 1709, well before the discovery of these marriage records, gave Anne's name as Hathaway.) The problems of marriage with Anne Hathaway — he was eighteen and she was twenty-six — and of the bond have caused similar consternation. Why did these two marry when there was such a discrepancy of age? Why only one saying of the banns (rather than the usual three)? Why the emphasis on a possible legal impediment? The answer here is not simple or definite, but the birth of a daughter Susanna, baptized at Holy Trinity on May 26, 1583, seems to explain the odd circumstances. It should be recognized, however, that an engagement to marry was considered legally binding in those days (we still have breach-of-promise suits today) and that premarital relations were not unusual or frowned upon when an engagement had taken place. The circumstances already mentioned, Shakespeare's ensuing activities, and his will bequeathing to Anne "my second best bed with the furniture" have suggested to some that their marriage was not entirely happy. Their other children, the twins Hamnet and Judith, were christened on February 2, 1585.

Theatrical Life

Shakespeare's years before and immediately after the time of his marriage are not charted, but rumor has him as an apprentice to a master butcher or as a country teacher or an actor with some provincial company. He is supposed to have run away from whatever he was doing for livelihood and to have gone to London, where he soon attached himself to some theatrical group. At this time there were only two professional houses established in the London environs, The Theatre (opened in 1576) and The Curtain (opened in 1577). His first connection with the theater was reputedly as holder of horses; that is, one of the stage crew, but a most inferior assignment. Thereafter he became an actor (perhaps at this time he met Ben Jonson), a writer, and a director. Such experience had its mark in the theatricality of his plays. We do know that he was established in London by 1592, when Robert Greene lamented in *A Groatsworth of Wit* (September, 1592) that professional actors had gained priority in the theater over university-trained writers like himself: "There is an upstart Crow, beautified with our feathers, that with his *Tygers hart wrapt in a Players hyde*, supposes he is as well able to bombast out a lanke verse as the best of you: and beeing an absolute *Iohannes fac totum* (Jack-of-all-trades), is in his owne conceit the onely Shake-scene in a countrey." An apology for Greene's ill-humored statement by Henry Chettle, the editor of the pamphlet, appeared around December 1592 in *Kind-Hart's Dream*.

Family Affairs

To return to the known details of family life, Shakespeare's son Hamnet was buried at Stratford on August 11, 1596; his father was given a coat of arms on October 20, 1596; and he purchased New Place (a refurbished tourist attraction today) on May 4, 1597. The London playwright obviously had not severed connections with his birthplace, and he was reflecting his new affluence by being known as William Shakespeare of Stratford-upon-Avon, in the County of Warwick, Gentleman. His father was buried in Stratford on September 8, 1601; his mother, on September 9, 1608. His daughter Susanna married Dr. John Hall on June 5, 1607, and they had a child named Elizabeth. His other daughter, Judith, married Thomas Quiney on February 10, 1616, without special licence, during Lent and was thus excommunicated. Shakespeare revised his will on March 25, 1616, and was buried on April 25, 1616 (according to the parish register). A monument by Gerard Janssen was erected in the Holy Trinity chancel in 1623 but many, like Milton several years later, protested:

> What needs my *Shakespeare* for his honour'd Bones,
> The labour of an age in piled Stone, . . .
> Thou in our wonder and astonishment
> Hast built thy self a live-long Monument.

Shakespeare's Writings

Order of Appearance

Dating of Shakespeare's early plays, while based on inconclusive evidence, has tended to hover around the early 1590's. Almost certainly it is his chronicles of Henry the Sixth that Philip Henslowe, an important theatrical manager of the day, referred to in his diary as being performed during March-May, 1592. An allusion to these plays also occurs in Thomas Nashe's *Piers Penniless His Supplication to the Devil* (August, 1592). Greene's quotation about a tiger is a paraphrase of "O tiger's heart wrapt in a woman's hide" from *Henry VI*, Part III.

The first published work to come from Shakespeare's hand was *Venus and Adonis* (1593), a long stanzaic poem, dedicated to Henry

Wriothesley, Earl of Southampton. A year later *The Rape of Lucrece* appeared, also dedicated to Southampton. Perhaps poetry was pursued during these years because the London theaters were closed as a result of a virulent siege of plague. The *Sonnets*, published in 1609, may owe something to Southampton, who had become Shakespeare's patron. Perhaps some were written as early as the first few years of the 1590's. They were mentioned (along with a number of plays) in 1598 by Francis Meres in his *Palladis Tamia*, and sonnets 138 and 144 were printed without authority by William Jaggard in *The Passionate Pilgrim* (1599).

There is a record of a performance of *A Comedy of Errors* at Gray's Inn (one of the law colleges) on December 28, 1594, and, during early 1595, Shakespeare was paid, along with the famous actors Richard Burbage and William Kempe, for performances before the Queen by the Lord Chamberlain's Men, a theatrical company formed the year before. The company founded the Globe Theatre on the south side of the Thames in 1599 and became the King's Men when James ascended the throne. Records show frequent payments to the company through its general manager John Heminge. From 1595 through 1614 there are numerous references to real estate transactions and other legal matters, to many performances, and to various publications connected with Shakespeare.

Order of Publication

The first plays to be printed were *Titus Andronicus* around February, 1594, and the garbled versions of *Henry VI*, Parts II and III in 1594. (Some scholars, however, question whether the last two are versions of *Henry VI*, Parts II and III, and some dispute Shakespeare's authorship.) Thereafter *Richard III* appeared in 1597 and 1598; *Richard II*, in 1597 and twice in 1598; *Romeo and Juliet*, in 1597 (a pirated edition) and 1599, and many others. Some of the plays appear in individual editions, with or without Shakespeare's name on the title page,but eighteen are known only from their appearance in the first collected volume (the so-called First Folio) of 1623. The editors were Heminge and Henry Condell, another member of Shakespeare's company. *Pericles* was omitted from the First Folio although it had appeared in 1609, 1611, and 1619; it was added to the Third Folio in 1664.

There was reluctance to publish plays at this time for various reasons; many plays were carelessly written for fast production; collaboration was frequent; plays were not really considered *reading* matter; they were sometimes circulated in manuscript; and the theatrical company, not the author, owned the rights. Those plays given individual publication appeared in a quarto, so named from the size of the page. A single sheet of paper was folded twice to make four leaves (thus *quarto*) or eight pages; these four leaves constitute one signature (one section of a bound book). A page measures about 6¾ in. x 8½ in. On the other hand, a folio sheet is folded once to make two leaves or four pages; three sheets, or twelve pages, constitute a signature. The page is approximately 8½ in. x 13⅜ in.

Authorized publication occurred when a company disbanded, when money was needed but rights were to be retained, when a play failed or ran into licensing difficulties (thus, hopefully, the printed work would justify the play against the criticism), or when a play had been pirated. Authorized editions are called good quartos. Piratical publication might occur when the manuscript of a play had circulated privately, when a member of a company desired money for himself, or when a stenographer or memorizer took the play down in the theater (such a version was recognizable by inclusion of stage directions derived from an eyewitness, by garbled sections, etc.). Pirated editions are called bad quartos; there are at least five bad quartos of Shakespeare's plays.

Authenticity of Works

Usually thirty-seven plays are printed in modern collections of Shakespeare's works but some recent scholars have urged the addition of two more: *Edward III* and *Two Noble Kinsmen*. A case has also been advanced, unconvincingly, for a fragment of the play on Sir Thomas More. At times, six of the generally-accepted plays have been questioned: *Henry VI*, Parts I, II and III, *Timon of Athens*, *Pericles* and *Henry VIII*. The first four are usually accepted today (one hopes all question concerning *Timon* has finally ended), but if Shakespeare did not write these plays in their entirety, he certainly wrote parts of them. Of course, collaboration in those days was commonplace. Aside from the two long narrative poems already mentioned and the sonnets (Nos. 1-152, but not Nos. 153-154), Shakespeare's poetic output is uncertain. *The Passionate Pilgrim* (1599) contains only five authenticated poems (two sonnets and three verses from *Love's Labour's Lost*); *The Phoenix and the Turtle* (1601) may be his, but the authenticity of *A Lover's Complaint* (appended to the sonnets) is highly questionable.

Who Was Shakespeare?

At this point we might mention a problem that has plagued Shakespeare study for over a century: who was Shakespeare? Those who would like to make the author of the plays someone else — Francis Bacon or the Earl of Oxford or even Christopher Marlowe (dead long before most of the plays were written) — have used the lack of information of Shakespeare's early years and the confusion in the evidence we have been examining to advance their candidate. But the major arguments against Shakespeare show the source of these speculators' disbelief to be in classconscious snobbery and perhaps in a perverse adherence to minority opinion. The most common argument is that no one of Shakespeare's background, lack of education, and lack of aristocratic experience could know all that the author knew. But study will reveal that such information was readily available in various popular sources, that some of it lies in the literary sources used for the play, and that Shakespeare was probably not totally lacking in education or in social decorum. The more significant question of style and tone is not dealt with — nor could it successfully be raised. Bacon, for example, no matter how much we admire his mind and his writings, exhibits a writing style diametrically opposite to Shakespeare's, a style most unpoetic and often flat. The student would be wise not to waste time rehashing these unfounded theories. No such question was raised in the seventeenth or eighteenth centuries, and no serious student of the plays today doubts that Shakespeare *was* Shakespeare.

Shakespeare's Plays

Exact dates for Shakespeare's plays remain a source of debate among scholars. The following serve only as a general frame of reference.

	COMEDIES	TRAGEDIES	HISTORIES
1591			Henry VI, Part I
1592	Comedy of Errors		Henry VI, Part II
1592	Two Gentlemen of Verona		Henry VI, Part III
1593	Love's Labour's Lost	Titus Andronicus	Richard III
1594			King John
1595	Midsummer Night's Dream	Romeo and Juliet	Richard II
1596	Merchant of Venice		
1596	Taming of the Shrew		
1597			Henry IV, Part I
1598	Much Ado About Nothing		Henry IV, Part II
1599	As You Like It	Julius Caesar	
1599	Merry Wives of Windsor		Henry V
1601	Twelfth Night	Hamlet	
1602	Troilus and Cressida		
1602	All's Well That Ends Well		
1604	Measure for Measure	Othello	
1605		King Lear	
1606		Macbeth	
1607		Timon of Athens	
1607		Antony and Cleopatra	
1608	Pericles		
1609		Coriolanus	
1610	Cymbeline		
1611	Winter's Tale		
1611	Tempest		
1613			Henry VIII

Shakespeare's England

The world of Elizabethan and Jacobean England was a world of growth and change. The great increase in the middle class, and in the population as a whole, demanded a new economy and means of livelihood, a new instrument of government (one recognizing "rights" and changed class structure), a new social code and a broad base of entertainment. The invention of printing a century before had contributed to that broader base, but it was the theater that supplied the more immediate needs of the greatest numbers. The theater grew and along with it came less-educated, more money-conscious writers, who gave the people what they wanted: entertainment. But Shakespeare, having passed through a brief period of hack writing, proceeded to set down important ideas in memorable language throughout most of his career. His plays, particularly the later ones, have been analyzed by recent critics in terms of literary quality through their metaphor, verse-line, relationships with psychology and myth, and elaborate structure. Yet Shakespeare was a man of the stage, and the plays were written to be performed. Only this will fully account for the humor of a deadly serious play like *Hamlet* or the spectacle of a *Coriolanus*.

Life in London

During Shakespeare's early years there, London was a walled city of about 200,000, with seven gates providing access to the city from the east, north, and west. It was geographically small and crisscrossed by narrow little streets and lanes. The various wards each had a parish church that dominated the life of the close-knit community. To the south and outside were slums and the haunts of criminal types, and farther out were the agricultural lands and huge estates. As the population increased and the central area declined, the fashionable people of the city moved toward the west, where the palace of Westminster lay. Houses were generally rented out floor by floor and sometimes room by room. Slums were common within the city, too, though close to pleasant enough streets and squares. "Merrie Olde England" was not really clean, nor were its people, for in those days there were no sewers or drains except the gutter in the middle of the street, into which garbage would be emptied to be floated off by the rain to Fleet ditch or Moor ditch. Plague was particularly ravaging in 1592, 1593-94 (when the theaters were closed to avoid contamination) and 1603. Medical knowledge, of course, was slight; ills were "cured" by amputation, leeching, blood-letting and cathartics. The city was (and still is) dominated by St. Paul's Cathedral, around which booksellers clustered on Paternoster Row.

Religious Atmosphere

Of great significance for the times was religion. Under Elizabeth, a state church had developed; it was Protestant in nature and was called Anglican (or today, Episcopalian) but it had arisen from Henry VIII's break with the Pope and from a compromise with the Roman Catholics who had gained power under Mary Tudor.

The Church of England was headed by the Archbishop of Canter bury, who was to be an increasingly important figure in the early part of the seventeenth century. There were also many schismatic groups, which generally desired further departures from Roman Catholicism. Calvinists were perhaps the most numerous and important of the Protestant groups. The Puritans, who were Calvinist, desired to "purify" the church of ritual and certain dogmas, but during the 1590's they were lampooned as extremists in dress and conduct.

Political Milieu

During Shakespeare's lifetime there were two monarchs: Elizabeth, 1558-1603, and James I, 1603-1625. Elizabeth was the daughter of Henry VIII and Anne Boleyn, his second wife, who was executed in 1536. After Henry's death, his son by his third wife, Jane Seymore (died in 1537), reigned as Edward VI. He was followed by Mary Tudor, daughter of Henry's first wife, Catherine of Aragon. Mary was a Roman Catholic, who tried to put down religious dissension by persecution of both Protestants and Catholics. Nor did her marriage to Philip II of Spain endear her to the people.

Elizabeth's reign was troubled by many offers of marriage, particularly from Spanish and French nobles — all Roman Catholic — and by the people's concern for an heir to the throne. English suitors generally cancelled one another out by intrigue or aggressiveness. One of the most prominent was the Earl of Essex, Robert Devereux, who fell in and out of favor; he apparently attempted to take over the reins of control, only to be captured, imprisoned and executed in February, 1601. One claimant to the throne was Mary of Scotland, a Roman Catholic and widow of Francis II of France. She was the second cousin of Elizabeth, tracing her claim through her grandmother, who was Henry VIII's sister. Finally, settlement came with Elizabeth's acceptance of Mary's son as heir apparent, though Mary was to be captured, tried and executed for treason in 1587. Mary had abdicated the throne of Scotland in 1567 in favor of her son, James VI. His ascent to the throne of England in 1603 as James I joined the two kingdoms for the first time, although Scotland during the seventeenth century often acted independently of England.

Contemporary Events

Political and religious problems were intermingled in the celebrated Gunpowder Plot. Angry over fines that were levied upon those not attending Church of England services — primarily Roman Catholics — and offended by difficulties over papal envoys, a group of Catholics plotted to blow up Parliament, and James with it, at its first session on November 5, 1605. A cache of gunpowder was stored in the cellar, guarded by various conspirators, among them Guy Fawkes. The plot was discovered before it could be carried out and Fawkes, on duty at the time, was apprehended. The execution of the plotters and the triumph of the anti-Papists led in succeeding years to celebrations in the streets and the hanging of Fawkes in effigy.

Among the most noteworthy public events during these times were the wars with the Spanish, which included the defeat of the Spanish Armada in 1588, the battle in the Lowlands in 1590-1594, the expedition to Cadiz under Essex in 1596 and the expedition to the Azores (the Islands Expedition), also under Essex, in 1597. With trading companies especially set up for colonization and exploitation, travel excited the imagination of the people: here was a new way of life, here were new customs brought back by the sailors and merchants, here was a new dream world to explore.

In all, the years from around 1590 to 1601 were trying ones for English people, relieved only by the news from abroad, the new affluence and the hope for the future under James. Writers of the period frequently reflect, however, the disillusionment and sadness of those difficult times.

The Elizabethan Theater

Appearance

The Elizabethan playhouse developed from the medieval inn with its rooms grouped around a courtyard into which a stage was built. This pattern was used in The Theatre, built by James Burbage in 1576: a square frame building (later round or octagonal) with a square yard, three tiers of galleries, each jutting out over the one below, and a stage extending into the middle of the yard, where people stood or sat on improvised seats. There was no cover over the yard or stage and lighting was therefore natural. Thus performances were what we might consider late matinees or early evening performances; in summer, daylight continues in London until around ten o'clock.

Other theaters were constructed during the ensuing years: The Curtain in 1577, The Rose in 1587 (on Bankside), The Swan in 1595 (also Bankside) and Shakespeare's playhouse, The Globe, in 1599 (not far from The Rose). There is still some question about the exact dimensions of this house, but it seems to have been octagonal, each side measuring about 36 feet, with an over-all diameter of 84 feet. It was about 33 feet to the eaves, and the yard was 56 feet in diameter. Three sides were used for backstage and to serve the needs of the players. There was no curtain or proscenium, hence the spectators became part of the action. Obviously, the actors' asides and soliloquies were effective under these conditions.

There was no real scenery and there were only a few major props; thus the lines of the play had to reveal locations and movement, changes in time or place, etc. In this way, too, it was easier to establish a nonrealistic setting, for all settings were created in words. On either side of the stage were doors, within the flooring were trapdoors (for entrances of ghosts, etc.), and behind the main stage was the inner stage or recess. Here, indoor scenes (such as a court or a bedchamber) were played, and some props could be used because the inner stage was usually concealed by a curtain when not in use. It might also have served to hide someone behind the ever-present arras, like Polonius in *Hamlet*. The "chamber" was on the second level, with windows and a balcony. On the third level was another chamber, primarily for musicians.

Actors

An acting company such as the Lord Chamberlain's Men was a fellowship of ten to fifteen sharers with some ten to twelve extras, three or four boys (often to play women's roles) who might become full sharers, and stagehands. There were rival companies, each with its leading dramatist and leading tragic actor and clown. The Lord Admiral's Men, organized in 1594, boasted Ben Jonson and the tragedian Edward Alleyn. Some of the rivalry of this War of the Theaters is reflected in the speeches of Hamlet, who also comments on the ascendancy and unwarranted popularity of the children's companies (like the Children of Blackfriars) in the late 1590's.

The company dramatist, of course, had to think in terms of the members of his company as he wrote his play. He had to make use of the physical features and peculiar talents of the actors, making sure, besides, that there was a role for each member. The fact that women's parts were taken by boys imposed obvious limitations on the range of action. Accordingly, we often find women characters impersonating men; for example, Robert Goffe played Portia in *The Merchant of Venice*, and Portia impersonates a male lawyer in the important trial scene. Goffe also played Juliet, and Anne in *Richard III*, and Oberon in *Midsummer Night's Dream*. The influence of an actor on the playwright can be seen, on the one hand, by noting the "humor" characters portrayed so competently by Thomas Pope, who was a choleric Mercutio in *Romeo*, a melancholic Jaques in *As You Like It*, and a sanguinary Falstaff in *Henry IV*, Part I; and by comparing, on the other hand, the clown Bottom in *Midsummer Night's Dream*, played in a frolicsome manner by William Kempe, with the clown Feste in *Twelfth Night*, sung and danced by Robert Armin. Obviously, too, if a certain kind of character was not available within the company, then that kind of character could not be written into the play. The approach was decidedly different from ours today, where the play almost always comes first and the casting of roles second. The plays were performed in a repertory system, with a different play each afternoon. The average life of a play was about ten performances.

History of the Drama

English drama goes back to native forms developed from playlets presented at Church holidays. Mystery plays dealt with biblical stories such as the Nativity or the Passion, and miracle plays usually depicted the lives of saints. The merchant and craft guilds that came to own and produce the cycles of plays were the forerunners of the theatrical companies of Shakespeare's time. The kind of production these cycles received, either as moving pageants in the streets or as staged shows in a churchyard, influenced the late sixteenth-century production of a secular play: there was an intimacy with the audience and there was a great reliance on words rather than setting and props. Similar involvement with the stage action is experienced by audiences of the arena theater of today.

The morality play, the next form to develop, was an allegory of the spiritual conflict between good and evil in the soul of man. The *dramatis personae* were abstract virtues and vices, with at least one man representing Mankind (or Everyman, as the most popular of these plays was titled). Some modern critics see *Othello* as a kind of morality play in which the soul of Othello is vied for by the aggressively evil Iago (as a kind of Satanic figure) and passively good Desdemona (as a personification of Christian faith in all men). The Tudor interlude — a short, witty, visual play — may have influenced the subplot of the Elizabethan play with its low-life and jesting and visual tricks. In mid-sixteenth century appeared the earliest known English comedies, Nicholas Udall's *Ralph Roister Doister* and *Gammer Gurton's Needle* (of uncertain authorship). Both show the influence of the Roman comic playwright Plautus. Shakespeare's *Comedy of Errors*, performed in the 1590's, was an adaptation of Plautus' *Menaechmi*, both plays featuring twins and an involved story of confused identities. The influence of the Roman tragedian Seneca can be traced from Thomas Norton and Thomas Sackville in *Gorboduc* to *Hamlet*. Senecan tragedy is a tragedy of revenge, characterized by many deaths, much blood-letting, ghosts, feigned madness and the motif of a death for a death.

Shakespeare's Artistry

Plots

Generally, a Shakespearean play has two plots: a main plot and a subplot. The subplot reflects the main plot and is often concerned with inferior characters. Two contrasting examples will suffice: Lear and his daughters furnish the characters for the main plot of filial love and ingratitude, whereas Gloucester and his sons enact the same theme in the subplot; Lear and Gloucester both learn that outward signs of love may be false. In *Midsummer Night's Dream*, the town workmen (Quince, Bottom *et al.*) put on a tragic play in such a hilarious way that it turns the subject of the play — love so strong that the hero will kill himself if his loved one dies first — into farce, but this in the main plot is the "serious" plight of the four mixed-up lovers. In both examples Shakespeare has reinforced his points by subplots dealing with the same subject as the main plot.

Sources

The plots of the Elizabethan plays were usually adapted from other sources. "Originality" was not the sought quality; a kind of variation on a theme was. It was felt that one could better evaluate the playwright's worth by seeing what he did with a familiar tale. What he stressed, how he stressed it, how he restructured the familiar elements — these were the important matters. Shakespeare closely followed Sir Thomas North's very popular translation of Plutarch's *Life of Marcus Antonius*, for example, in writing *Antony and Cleopatra*; and he modified Robert Greene's *Pandosto* and combined it with the Pygmalion myth in *The Winter's Tale*, while drawing the character of Autolycus from certain pamphlets written by Greene. The only plays for which sources have not been clearly determined are *Love's Labour's Lost* (probably based on contemporary events) and *The Tempest* (possibly based on some shipwreck account from travellers to the New World).

Verse and Prose

There is a mixture of verse and prose in the plays, partially because plays fully in verse were out of fashion. Greater variety could thus be achieved and character or atmosphere could be more precisely delineated. Elevated passages, philosophically significant ideas, speeches by men of high rank are in verse, but comic and light parts, speeches including dialect or broken English, and scenes that move more rapidly or simply give mundane information are in prose. The poetry is almost always blank verse (iambic pentameter lines without rhyme). Rhyme is used, however (particularly the couplet), to mark the close of scenes or an important action. Rhyme also serves as a cue for the entrance of another actor or some off-stage business, to point to a change of mood or thought, as a forceful opening after a passage of prose, to convey excitement or passion or sentimentality and to distinguish characters.

Shakespeare's plays may be divided into three general categories, though some plays are not readily classified and further subdivisions may be suggested within a category.

The History Play

The history play, or chronicle, may tend to tragedy, like *Richard II*, or to comedy, like *Henry IV*, Part I. It is a chronicle of some royal personage, often altered for dramatic purposes, even to the point of falsification of the facts. Its popularity may have resulted from the rising of nationalism of the English, nurtured by their successes against the Spanish, their developing trade and colonization, and their rising prestige as a world power. The chronicle was considered a political guide, like the popular *Mirror for Magistrates*, a collection of writings showing what happens when an important leader falls through some error in his ways, his thinking or his personality. Thus the history play counseled the right path by negative, if not positive, means. Accordingly, it is difficult to call *Richard II* a tragedy, since Richard was wrong and his wrongness harmed his people. The political philosophy of Shakespeare's day seemed to favor the view that all usurpation was bad and should be corrected, but not by further usurpation. When that original usurpation had been established, through an heir's ascension to the throne, it was to be accepted. Then any rebellion against the "true" king would be a rebellion against God.

Tragedy

Tragedy in simple terms meant that the protagonist died. Certain concepts drawn from Aristotle's *Poetics* require a tragic hero of high standing, who must oppose some conflicting force, either external or internal. The tragic hero should be dominated by a *hamartia* (a so-called tragic flaw, but really an *excess* of some character trait, e.g., pride, or *hubris*), and it is this *hamartia* that leads to his downfall and, because of his status, to the downfall of others. The action presented in the tragedy must be recognizable to the audience as real and potential: through seeing it enacted, the audience has its passion (primarily suffering) raised, and the conclusion of the action thus brings release from that passion (*catharsis*). A more meaningful way of looking at tragedy in the Elizabethan theater, however, is to see it as that which occurs when essential good (like Hamlet) is wasted (through disaster or death) in the process of driving out evil (such as Claudius represents).

Comedy

Comedy in simple terms meant that the play ended happily for the protagonists. Sometimes the comedy depends on exaggerations of man's eccentricities — comedy of humors; sometimes the comedy is romantic and far-fetched. The romantic comedy was usually based on a mix-up in events or confused identity of characters, particularly by disguise. It moved toward tragedy in that an important person might die and the mix-up might never be unraveled; but in the nick of time something happens or someone appears (sometimes illogically or unexpectedly) and saves the day. It reflects the structure of myth by moving from happiness to despair to resurrection. *The Winter's Tale* is a perfect example of this, for the happiness of the first part is banished with Hermione's exile and Perdita's abandonment; tragedy is near when the lost baby, Perdita, cannot be found and Hermione is presumed dead, but Perdita reappears, as does Hermione, a statue that suddenly comes to life. Lost identities are established and confusions disappear but the mythic-comic nature of the play is seen in the reuniting of the mother, Hermione, a kind of Ceres, with her daughter, Perdita, a kind of Prosperina. Spring returns, summer will bring the harvest, and the winter of the tale is left behind — for a little while.

What is it, then, that makes Shakespeare's art so great? Perhaps we see in it a whole spectrum of humanity, treated impersonally, but with kindness and understanding. We seldom meet in Shakespeare a weeping philosopher: he may criticize, but he criticizes both sides. After he has done so, he gives the impression of saying, Well, that's the way life is; people will always be like that — don't get upset about it. This is probably the key to the Duke's behavior in *Measure for Measure* — a most unbitter comedy despite former labels. Only in *Hamlet* does Shakespeare not seem to fit this statement; it is the one play that Shakespeare, the person, enters.

As we grow older and our range of experience widens, so, too, does Shakespeare's range seem to expand. Perhaps this lies in the ambiguities of his own materials, which allow for numerous individual readings. We meet our own experiences — and they are ours alone, we think — expressed in phrases that we thought our own or of our own discovery. What makes Shakespeare's art so great, then, is his ability to say so much to so many people in such memorable language: he is himself "the show and gaze o' the time."

HENRY IV, PART I

Background

One of Shakespeare's aims in writing this play was to follow up his previous success with *Richard II*, which may well be regarded as the forerunner of *Henry IV*, Part I. This play was followed by *Henry IV*, Part II, and by *Henry V*, thus completing the cycle. Several incidents referred to in *Richard II* crop up again in *Henry IV*, Part I, and the central figure, Henry Bolingbroke, is common to both; the Prince Hal of *Henry IV*, Part I is the monarch in *Henry V*. Shakespeare probably did not originally intend to write a series of historical plays neatly fitting together in this manner, since *Richard II* is very different in tone and treatment from the other plays in what did, in effect, become a series.

In the play, *Richard II*, Henry Bolingbroke, son and heir of John of Gaunt (son of Edward III) accuses Thomas Mowbray (Duke of Norfolk) of treason. They are about to settle the matter by personal combat when King Richard intervenes and banishes them both from his kingdom. Mowbray is banished for life, Bolingbroke for only six years: this action shows whom the king favored. King Richard confiscates all John of Gaunt's lands and revenues when the noble old man dies (after rebuking Richard for his poor housekeeping, which is likely to bankrupt the kingdom, "this royal throne of kings"), then sets sail for Ireland to crush a rebellion there. In his absence, Richard's uncle (the Duke of York) is appointed protector of the kingdom, and the Earl of Northumberland and his impetuous son, Hotspur, stay behind because they suspect that Bolingbroke will soon be returning to claim his father's (i.e., John of Gaunt's) lands and revenues.

Henry Bolingbroke lands at Ravenspurgh (a port which actually existed, but which has since been silted up) and is met by Northumberland, and later by York and Hotspur. He swears that he has come back only to claim the property that has been wrongly taken from him, together with the Dukedom of Lancaster to which he is now entitled, but it soon becomes clear that he is after the crown of England. The common people acclaim him, and he makes his way amid an enthusiastic throng who encourage him to take power. Richard hurries back from Ireland to find himself deserted and betrayed. He surrenders to Bolingbroke, and is retired to Pomfret Castle, where he is murdered shortly after by Sir Pierce Exton, at the request of the new king. Richard's murder at Pomfret marks the climax of the play *Richard II*, and Henry Bolingbroke becomes the reigning monarch (Henry IV) of *Henry IV*, Part I. This king's son is the reigning monarch (Henry V) of *Henry IV*, Part II and, of course, of *Henry V*. In *Henry IV*, Part I he is called Prince Hal (or Prince of Wales).

In studying *Henry IV*, Part I, it is helpful to keep in mind the following groups:

GROUP 1: THE ROYAL COURT (Henry IV and his followers).
GROUP 2: THE REBELS (Northumberland and Hotspur).
GROUP 3: THE COMIC CHARACTERS (Falstaff and the low-life characters).

These three groups are quite loosely interconnected in various ways, and the story of their interconnections constitutes the plot of the play. This play is much less compactly structured than the tragedies of Shakespeare, but provides us with some lovable characters, the most notable of whom is the immortal Falstaff. Nevertheless, though Falstaff is perhaps the most memorable and humorous character in this play, he is not the hero: this position is undoubtedly occupied by the prince. It is the prince's function to help *link* all three centers of interest in this play.

Date of Composition

In the First Folio of 1623, compiled by Shakespeare's friends after the playwright's death, the section made up of the so-called histories contained one play, the full title of which takes up several lines, namely: The History of Henrie The Fourth; With the Battell of Shrewsburie, Betweene the King and Lord Henry Percie Surnamed Henrie Hotspur of the North. With the Humorous Conceits of Sir John Falstalffe. This is the play that was probably first produced during the theatrical season of 1597-98.

The term "histories" was intended to distinguish those plays which deal with English history from other plays, usually tragedies, which take their plots from events in Greek or Roman history. But since there is much in *Henry IV*, Part I which is probably not true to history (the matter of historical accuracy is discussed later) it would, perhaps, be better to call this play a *chronicle*, or even a *pageant*. It is sometimes staged as a *tableau vivant* — that is, a living spectacle — but there is too much character play and character development to justify calling the play this.

The Elizabethans were used to chronicle plays, and liked them. Chronicle plays were, however, virtually unknown in Europe at this time. They usually consisted of mere successions of scenes dealing with some reign or episode in English history, with little or no attempt to mold the material obtained from the history books, or chronicles, into dramatic form. The chronicle plays were the chief means of communicating historical information to massive audiences, though they frequently and inevitably communicated political bias and gross distortions of truth as well. The documentary war film is the direct descendent of the chronicle plays of old, and it possesses their strengths and weaknesses.

It is not difficult to connect the chronicle play, especially its teaching and moralizing function, with the older morality plays, the most famous of which is *Everyman*. The Tudor period was interested in power politics centering upon the throne and its succession, and the historians whose ideas Shakespeare reflected in his plays believed that history should be represented to demonstrate moral instruction and guidance. This view of history has passed away in most western universities, but continues to be preached from the pulpit in many cases.

It was not enlightening for the Prince of Wales to spend so much time with rascals and knaves like Sir John Falstaff. But to show him playing a trick on Falstaff and then to show his conversion from knavery to dutifulness and responsibility is a profoundly moving moral spectacle. In this way, *Henry IV*, Part I belongs to the moral tradition of the ancient moralities. Yet its characterization is not as stiff, nor its scenes as disconnected, as the earlier three parts of *Henry VI*. It is a more coherent play than they, but not as coherent (in the structural and developmental senses) as the tragedies.

Sources

Before Shakespeare wrote *Henry IV*, Part I, an older play on the same period of English History had appeared, and was called *The Famous Victories of Henry the Fifth: containing the Honourable Battell of Agin-court*. It is clear that this older play was performed before 1588, as Richard Tarleton, a well-known actor, who had taken part in it, died in that year. The play, although it had been acted many times, was quite worthless, but it was, in fact, so popular that it was revived by Henslow's Company of Actors in 1595 and republished in 1598. Some of the incidents and the names of the characters in *Henry IV* are very similar to those used in the *Famous Victories*, and it may safely be assumed that not only was Shakespeare well acquainted with this earlier play, but he made use of it when writing *Henry IV*.

The main incidents and characters of the play were taken from Holinshed's *Chronicles of England, Scotland and Ireland*, which was first published in 1577. This was followed by a second and enlarged edition in 1587, which was undoubtedly that used by Shakespeare.

Below will be found a few short extracts from Holinshed, with the corresponding passage from Shakespeare. It is obvious to what a great extent Shakespeare made use of Holinshed.

(a) Owen Glendower, according to his accustomed manner, robbing and spoiling within the English borders, caused all the forces of the shire of Hereford to assemble together against them, under the conduct of Edmund Mortimer, earle of March. But coming to trie the matter by battell, whether by treason or otherwise, as it fortuned, that the English power was discomfited, the earle taken prisoner, and above a thousand of his people slaine in the place. The shamefull villanie used by the Welsh women towards the dead carcasses, was such, as honest eares would be ashamed to heare, and continent toongs to speake thereof.

A post from Wales loaden with heavy news,
Whose worst was that the noble Mortimer,
Leading the men of Herefordshire to fight
Against the irregular and wild Glendower,
Was by the rude hands of that Welshman taken,
A thousand of his people butchered;
Upon whose dead corpse there was such misuse,
Such beastly shameless transformation,
By those Welshwomen done as may not be
Without much shame retold or spoken of.

(Act I, Sc. 1, 37-46)

(b) For at a place called Homildon they were so fiercely assailed by the Englishmen under the leading of the lord Percie, surnamed Henrie Hotspur and George, earle of March, that with violence of the English shot they were quite vanquished and put to flight, on the Rood day in harvest, with a great slaughter made by the Englishmen.

There were slaine of estimation sir John Swinton, sir Adam Gordon, sir John Leviston, sir Alexander Ramsie of Dalehousie, and three and twenty knights, besides ten thousand of the Commons; and of prisoners among other were these — Mordacke earle of Fife, son to the governour Archembald earle Douglas, which in the fight lost one of his ies, Thomas earle of Murray, Robert earle of Angus, and (as some writers have) the earles of Atholl and Menteith, with five hundred other of meaner degrees.

For more uneven and unwelcome news
Came from the north, and thus it did import:
On Holy-rood Day, the gallant Hotspur there,
Young Harry Percy and brave Archibald,
That ever-valiant and approved Scot,
At Holmedon met, of prisoners, Hotspur took
Mordrake Earl of Fife and eldest son
To beaten Douglas, and the Earl of Athol,
Of Murray, Angus, and Menteith.
And is not this an honourable spoil?

(Act I, Sc. 1, 50-55; 70-74)

(c) Herewith, they by their deputies in the house of the archdeacon of Bangor, divided the realme amongst them, causing a tripartite indenture to be made and sealed with their seales, by the covenants thereof, all English from Severne and Trent, south and eastward, was assigned to the earle of March: all Wales and the lands beyond Severne westward were appointed to Owen Glendower: and all the remnant from Trent northward to the lord Persie.

Glendower: Come, here is the map. Shall we divide our right
According to our threefold order ta'en?
Mortimer: The archdeacon hath divided it
Into three limits very equally.
England, from Trent and Severn hitherto,
By south and east is to my part assigned;
All westward, Wales beyond the Severn shore,
And all the fertile land within that bound,
To Owen Glendower; and, dear coz, to you
The remnant northward, lying off from Trent.
And our indentures tripartite are drawn,
Which being sealed interchangeably,
(A business that this night may execute), . . .
(Act III, Sc. 1, 70-82)

The Text

Since Shakespeare wrote his plays for the immediate use of actors, he was concerned that they received a masterscript so that they could make copies of their own parts, with their cues. This copying was done hurriedly with little respect for punctuation, or even verbal or metrical accuracy. When the actor had learned his lines by heart, he frequently threw away the script. Later, if a script were needed for another actor, the words might be written out from memory by the actor who remembered them best. In this way, no accurate edition of the plays was available. In 1623, the First Folio was published by Shakespeare's friends and acquaintances who had to rely on actors' scripts and their own and others' memories. Some expert editing had to be done, and the problems of variant readings and scholarly preferences came into existence. Many Elizabethan plays (some famous ones too) were never printed at all, or have been lost. It is conceivable that some of Shakespeare's plays have been lost, and the possibility of making an important literary "find" remains to tantalize the book collectors and other literary antiquarians.

Historical Accuracy of the Play

Suppose that this play is found, after examination, to be historically inaccurate, and to contain and thereby perpetuate distortions and prejudices. This certainly does not mean that it is necessarily bad entertainment. We do not usually require stage plays and other forms of entertainment to be historically accurate. We do not object to comedians being wildly inaccurate when they present a skit on politics. Why, then, should we require historical accuracy in *Henry IV*, Part I? This play is called a history; but this simply means that it deals in a creative and imaginative manner with episodes taken from English history. There is no obligation on the writer to engage in detailed historical research to make sure that he has his facts right. Tudor historians favored the sweeping generalization, the anti-Richard, pro-Bolingbroke theme. They were pro-Henry IV (with few exceptions) and anti-Percy, and so, by and large, were most Elizabethans. So was Shakespeare, fortunately, for this attitude enabled him to give them a play reinforcing all their own prejudices, thereby insuring popularity and consequently a profitable box-office return.

Where, though, did Shakespeare take liberties with his source material and, therefore, with historical fact and interpretation? In the first place, he juggled ages. In the play, Prince Hal and Hotspur are the same age; this similarity is pleasing to an audience naïve enough to prefer convenient but unlikely parallelisms of chronology. In fact (historically), Prince Hal was only fourteen years old while Hotspur was middle-aged. But if Shakespeare had left it at that, we would have been spared those flattering comparisons, all the suspense, and finally the exciting combat on the battlefield. The dramatic balance of this play actually depends on the parallelism of ages between the prince and Hotspur. King Henry IV had to be years older than the two boys, yet historically we are told that Hotspur was two years older than the king. History is evidently no artist. It does not know how to tidy up the loose ends, but Shakespeare did.

Shakespeare had no scruples about advancing the age of King Henry IV; thus he makes the king speak like an old man, "crushing *our old limbs* in ungentle steel" when, at the time of the Battle of Shrewsbury, Bolingbroke was only in his thirties.

Shakespeare delays historical episodes to suit his own dramatic purposes; thus the meeting and reconciliation between King Henry IV and Prince Hal takes place earlier in Holinshed's *Chronicles* than it does in *Henry IV*, Part I. This delay is needed to give the prince time to play the trick on Falstaff, and to play out the king's wrath with Falstaff after the lying episode. Since the reconciliation is the turning point of the play, it was necessary to precede it with some action to preserve the dramatic balance of the whole.

There is some uncertainty in the old writers about whether the king was rescued from mortal combat during the Battle of Shrewsbury, or whether he freed himself, or, if he was rescued, exactly who did the rescuing. Yet Shakespeare makes the prince rescue his father, thus placing Hal in a heroic light.

Shakespeare did not trouble himself to research details concerning where meetings took place. The meeting between Henry IV and Hotspur takes place in London, in the play; but actually it was held at Windsor Castle.

Shakespeare confuses two characters who have the same name, but so does Holinshed. Historically there were two Edmund Mortimers: the young Edmund Mortimer, Hotspur's brother-in-law, is confused with that Edmund Mortimer who was Earl of March. It was this Earl, rather than Hotspur's brother-in-law, whom Richard proclaimed heir to the English throne.

Shakespeare often transposes dates. The proposed crusade is placed by Shakespeare shortly after Henry IV's ascent to the throne, whereas in fact it took place during the final year of his reign.

Shakespeare absents Owen Glendower and the Welsh soldiery from the Battle of Shrewsbury in order to further weaken the rebel cause and hasten the victory of Henry IV; yet Holinshed states that the Welsh were present. The historian, Daniel, disagrees, and Shakespeare follows Daniel (or takes the initiative himself for internally satisfying dramatic reasons).

Prince John, Hal's younger brother, is introduced by Shakespeare as a suitable foil or contrast to the prince; yet, historically, Prince John must have been scarcely out of the cradle at this time.

Owen Glendower was probably not as visionary a Celt as he is made to seem by Shakespeare in this play, but Shakespeare seems to have based his character on that of the ancient magician, Merlin, in order to suit his plot. Besides, in this way Shakespeare further establishes the contrast between Glendower and his imaginativeness and caution, and Hotspur and his unimaginative, unreflecting impetuosity.

In the play, the prince refunds the money stolen by him from Falstaff, and by Falstaff from the stagecoach travellers, but he did no such thing according to Stow's version.

According to Shakespeare, King Henry IV was as generous to a defeated foe as he was towards the rebels; but according to history, Hotspur's body was crushed between millstones and, afterwards, quartered.

In all these respects, Shakespeare is inaccurate historically, but all of the changes are justified in terms of playwright's and poet's license.

Genealogical Chart

This much-simplified chart shows only those relationships among the descendants of Edward III which have some bearing on the action of *Henry IV*, Part I. Capital letters distinguish the names of people who actually appear in this play.

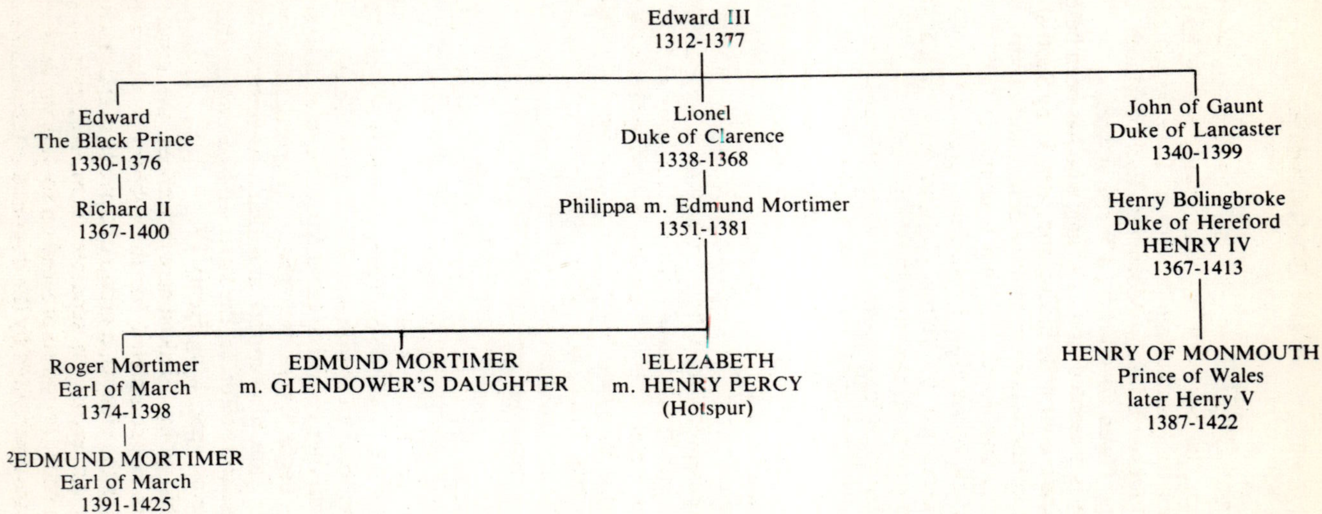

1 Called Kate in the play.
2 Shakespeare merges the identity of the two Edmund Mortimers. Holinshed, Shakespeare's source, makes the same error.

Plot Summary

The main plot of *Henry IV*, Part I has as its subject the rebellion of the Percies, the northern baronial family which had helped Henry depose Richard II and attain the crown. They are joined by the Scottish Earl of Douglas, Edmund Mortimer, Earl of March, claimant to the throne, and Owen Glendower, a Welsh noble.

Henry is presented first as a ruler who has been beset with troubles from the start: civil strife in England, attacks by Scottish forces moving across the northern border, and the defeat and capture of the still loyal Mortimer by Glendower. He thus is unable to fulfil his earlier vow to lead a crusade to the Holy Land. But there is one piece of good news: English forces led by young Hotspur have defeated the Scots at Holmedon and have captured the renowned Earl of Douglas. Yet this gives the harassed king reason to regret the irresponsibility of his son and heir, Prince Henry, who deliberately has avoided the court and public responsibility and spends his time in the company of the elderly, high-spirited Sir John Falstaff, as well as the lowly customers of the Boar's-Head Tavern in Eastcheap.

The comic subplot deals most amusingly with this same Falstaff and his companions, including Prince Hal, as he is appropriately called in this setting. In the initial episode, Hal joins with Poins, Bardolph, and Peto in a plan to trick Falstaff by having him participate in a robbery at Gad's Hill, be robbed in turn, and finally exposed as a coward and liar. Alone, Prince Hal soliloquizes, letting the audience know that, although he now chooses to enjoy himself in riotous company, he has no illusions about the character of his associates and will redeem himself publicly at the proper time.

The main plot takes precedence at this point. Once more at the court, King Henry confronts the Percies — Northumberland, Worcester, and Hotspur. He sternly reprimands them and demands to be told why the ranking Scottish prisoners taken by Hotspur have not been turned over to the crown. The Percies, deeply resenting the fact that the man they helped to the throne now intends to enforce absolute obedience, begin to plot their revolt. They will make peace with Glendower and gain his support and that of Mortimer. Then, aided by Welsh and Scottish forces, the latter led by Douglas, they will wage war against the usurper, King Henry IV.

At this point Shakespeare advances the comic subplot. Arrangements are completed for the robbery at Gad's Hill during the night. When the victims, a group of travellers, approach, Poins and the prince use an excuse to separate themselves from Falstaff and the others. Falstaff, forced to proceed on foot, is the leader of the robbers, who then are confronted by the disguised prince and Poins, and robbed in turn. Falstaff exhibits almost miraculous sluggishness in beating a retreat.

Again the action shifts to the main plot, wherein Hotspur is presented reading a letter from an English noble whose aid he has requested. He can hardly contain himself as he reads the excuses offered, and he condemns the writer as a coward. Then, in an exchange with his attractive young wife, Kate, he reveals himself as a man practically obsessed with matters relating solely to the planned revolt against the crown.

In Eastcheap at the Boar's-Head Tavern, Falstaff is exposed as the dupe who has been tricked by the prince and Poins. But, not unexpectedly in view of his already demonstrated wit, he not only survives the ordeal of being called a coward and liar, but emerges comically triumphant. Prior to all this, Hal had made satiric reference to the skill of Hotspur; now an emissary from the king informs Hal that he must appear at court promptly. This turn of events provides the prince with the opportunity to participate with Falstaff in a "play extempore," each successively enacting the role of King Henry scolding the wayward son and heir.

At the residence of the Archdeacon in North Wales, Hotspur, Worcester, Mortimer, and Glendower hold a parley, one not without some disagreement. They plan the campaign against the royal forces and the later division of England into three parts. The absence of the Earl of Northumberland is significant in light of later events.

In the meantime, we turn to the confrontation between the king and Prince Hal, in which the former compares his son unfavorably to the valiant Hotspur. But when Hal soberly vows to redeem his tarnished reputation at Hotspur's expense, the king not only forgives him but places him in command of royal forces. At that very moment the two learn that the rebels will be assembled at Shrewsbury.

Once more the action shifts to the Boar's-Head Tavern, where Falstaff is enjoying the company of Bardolph and Mistress Quickly. The prince and Peto arrive, and we learn that Hal has reimbursed the travellers who had been robbed at Gad's Hill and has arranged for Falstaff's commission as a leader of the king's forces.

Hotspur, Worcester, and Douglas learn that the Earl of Northumberland and his retainers will not join them. Apparently, illness has incapacitated him. Not for long is Hotspur dejected by this bad news. Sure of victory, he sees this as providing a greater opportunity to impress the multitude, whose support the rebels must gain and retain. Vernon arrives with the news that the royal army has set forth for Shrewsbury and that second in command to the king himself is the Prince of Wales. Hotspur, at first depressed by Vernon's glowing description of Hal, quickly recovers himself and declares that he will oppose the prince in single combat. Yet a third report is received: Glendower will require fourteen days to raise a force of Welshmen. But nothing can dampen the zeal nor restrain the impetuosity of Hotspur.

Now we meet Falstaff as a military commander. Unscrupulously he has managed to enlist a group of pitiful, physically unfit "soldiers" whom he will lead to Shrewsbury. Both Prince Hal and Westmoreland remark on their unfitness, but do nothing to stop Falstaff.

Sir Walter Blunt, a messenger from King Henry, arrives in the rebel camp and addresses the rebel leaders, voicing the orthodox condemnation of their disloyalty and conveying to them the king's willingness to listen to their grievances. Hotspur restates the rebel's arguments, and the royal offer is rejected.

In Yorkshire, the Archbishop of York and one Sir Michael, both in sympathy with the rebellious Percies, discuss the impending battle at Shrewsbury. Learning that Mortimer and his battle forces will not be able to join the rebels, the archbishop expresses his deep concern for the success of the enterprise. He directs Sir Michael to leave at once to enlist support, for he knows that King Henry, aware of his disloyalty, will move against him "if Lord Percy thrive not."

The action now moves to the king's camp at Shrewsbury. There, Worcester and Vernon meet with Henry IV, are given a chance once more to voice their grievances, are lectured on the subject of loyalty, and are offered generous terms if they will disband their forces. Prince Hal speaks words of praise for Hotspur, modestly admits that he himself has been irresponsible, and offers to fight his rival in single combat. The two rebel leaders depart, apparently to report to Hotspur what has been said by the king and prince. Present during all this was Sir John Falstaff, who, left to himself, soliloquizes on the impractical aspects of heroism and honor.

Worcester does not tell his nephew about the king's offer, convinced that under any circumstances the older leaders of the revolt will be the objects of Henry's wrath. But Vernon reports honestly and clearly to Hotspur how Prince Hal conducted himself. When a messenger announces the approach of the royal forces, Hotspur sounds the call to battle.

In the course of that battle, Douglas slays Blunt, mistaking him for the king, and he exchanges words of warlike determination with Hotspur. A contrast is provided by Falstaff, who suddenly appears after the two have left. We learn that he has committed his tattered troops to battle, wherein they, with the exception of one or two, have been slaughtered. When the prince appears, deadly serious, Falstaff employs his verbal wit once more — and is soundly criticized.

Prince Hal rescues his father from the sword of Douglas, and meets and kills his great rival, Hotspur. After the prince's departure for another part of the battlefield, Falstaff reappears. Then, when Hal returns with his brother, Prince John of Lancaster, Falstaff claims to have killed the young rebel leader. Neither of the princes bothers to deny his claim at any length. Worcester and Vernon are captured and later put to death. But Douglas, also a captive, is set free by the generous Prince Hal. The rebel forces have been badly defeated. King Henry then sends John of Lancaster to the north, where he will oppose Northumberland and the Archbishop Scroop; he himself will leave with Prince Hal to fight the forces led by Glendower and Mortimer.

Summaries and Commentaries by Act and Scene

ACT I • SCENE 1

Summary

At court, King Henry IV, shaken and exhausted by civil war, bids his followers enjoy a hard-won, but temporary, peace. The land, he says, is still divided. Thus, partly in order to unify his people and partly to fulfil his chivalric obligations as a medieval monarch, he plans to lead a crusade to the Holy Land. The discussion of this plan is interrupted, however, by Westmoreland, who brings news that Edmund Mortimer has been captured fighting for the king against the Welsh leader, Owen Glendower. But, Westmoreland informs us, on the happier side, that young Henry Percy (nicknamed Hotspur) has defeated the Earl of Douglas, leader of the Scottish rebels, a powerful warrior. We also learn that a number of notable prisoners have been taken. The king sadly comments on the difference between the brave, honorable young Hotspur and his own son, the Prince of Wales, who, rather than spend time on the field of battle, behaves irresponsibly and frequents taverns with disreputable companions. The king half wishes that the prince and Hotspur had been exchanged at birth, and that Hotspur were really his son. But, he observes, Hotspur has refused to fulfil his knightly obligation to turn his prisoners over to the king. Westmoreland suggests that this refusal results from the advice of the Earl of Worcester, Hotspur's conniving and ambitious uncle. The king angrily instructs that Hotspur be sent for.

Commentary

The play's opening scene introduces most of the themes important to the historical portions of the play. The condition of a land torn by seemingly continuous civil strife is described, and the hope of unity to be achieved through a foreign venture, later to be successfully exploited by King Henry V, is set forth. The present king, however, has a reason for planning a crusade, beyond the desire to unify the land. Such an obviously religious venture may help cleanse him of the sin involved in his deposition of his cousin, King Richard II. That this crime is, in large measure, the cause of Henry's unending problems will be suggested repeatedly throughout the play. The Edmund Mortimer affair is also introduced, and few in an Elizabethan audience would not know that Mortimer had been named legal heir to the throne by Richard before his murder, and that the king is not entirely unhappy at the news of Mortimer's capture. The figure of the fierce and mystical Welshman, Owen Glendower, whom Hotspur is later to lampoon unmercifully, is mentioned for the first time here. But the most important figure discussed in the scene is the young Henry Percy, whose nickname, Hotspur, is as appropriate as any of the many nicknames used for the characters in history plays.

The fact that at the historical time of the play Hotspur was a good deal older than Prince Hal, older in fact than King Henry, would not have disturbed an Elizabethan audience. Such anachronisms as a similarity in age for Hal and Hotspur were common in Elizabethan history plays, especially when the author desired to stress a point which historical accuracy would have precluded. It is of basic importance to *Henry IV* that Hal and Hotspur be roughly the same age. Both are heroic types. Hotspur, as we shall see, represents a fading chivalric tradition. It is Hotspur's own great failing that he cannot or will not admit that the old chivalry can no longer guide and govern the lives of the nobility. The king, in mentioning that his own son, Prince Hal, is deficient in the chivalric qualities of Hotspur, is unwittingly revealing that he, too, is behind the times. The prince, so unfavorably described, is not so deficient in essential honor as he is convinced of the foolishness, superficiality and meaningless behavior in a courtly tradition which has produced little more than pointless warfare and bloodshed. More such warfare and bloodshed is predicted in the impending clash between the king and Hotspur.

Notes

Find we a time for frighted peace. . . The meaning is "Let us have peace for a while and recover breath to propose new wars abroad." King Henry's policy, as disclosed in this scene, was to put an end to civil war by embarking upon a crusade to the Holy Land, which he hoped would have the effect of drawing off the complaints of those at home.

No more the thirsty entrance . . . Shakespeare appears to have had in his mind a personification of England, whose porous soil was saturated with the blood of her children. The "thirsty entrance" thus represents the English ground that drank in the blood that was shed, and in this connection the expression "Shall daub her lips" is justified as part of the image.

Trenching war: Shakespeare has in mind the damage done to the countryside by war. Though the ravages of war were nothing in the days of

Henry IV compared with what they are in the present day, the digging of trenches and erection of earthworks would leave the inevitable scar.

Opposed eyes: An example of the figure of speech known as synecdoche: the part used to represent the whole. By "opposed eyes" Shakespeare means opposed armies.

All of one nature, of one substance bred . . . Fellow countrymen at present engaged in civil war. The general idea of this passage is that the two sections of the nation which are at present lined up in battle array, face to face, will face the same way and fight shoulder to shoulder if the king can arouse enthusiasm by another crusade to the Holy Land; thus may unity be attained.

As far as to the sepulchre of Christ . . . shall we levy, . . . To "levy" is to raise a force, and here the term is used to suggest not only the raising of the force, but the leading of it to Jerusalem.

Cousin: Shakespeare uses the word "cousin" to mean any degree of relationship, and it is frequently used by him, as in the present instance, as a courtesy title, since Ralph Neville, the Earl of Westmoreland, had no blood-relationship with King Henry IV. In this connection, it is interesting to note that King Henry V, the son of King Henry IV, addresses the same man as "my cousin Westmoreland."

Holy-rood Day: September 14th, on which day in the year 1402 was fought the battle of Holmedon or Halidown Hill in Northumberland.

Mordake, Earl of Fife and eldest son/To beaten Douglas: Mordake was son to the Duke of Albany, regent of Scotland, and not to the Earl of Douglas, a mistake which probably arose from a misinterpretation of a passage in Holinshed from which this account of the battle was taken.

ACT I • SCENE 2

Summary

Prince Hal and Falstaff are drinking in the prince's chambers. In response to Falstaff's innocent enough question as to the time of day, Hal asks him why he would possibly be concerned about the time,

> Unless hours were cups of sack [a strong variety of sherry wine], minutes capons, and clocks the tongues of bawds [keepers of a brothel], and dials the signs of leaping houses [brothels], and the blessed sun himself a fair hot wench in flame-colored taffeta, . . .
>
> (Act I, Sc. 2, 6-10)

Falstaff, changing the subject, assures him that the sun is of little concern to him since he works at night (stealing purses), and adds that he hopes when the prince is king, highwaymen and robbers will no longer be considered ne'er-do-wells. They exchange remarks, heavily loaded with puns, on the theme of Falstaff's crimes, the inevitability of his being hanged, and on the questionable relations both have had with the hostess of the tavern in Eastcheap (a run-down section of the city). Falstaff repeats the thought that when Hal is king, there will be no more hangings, that robbery and vice will not be hindered as it is now by "old father antic [crotchety old man] the law." Hal suggests that he will settle matters by making Falstaff hangman, which Falstaff thinks might be a good thing, since hangmen inherit their victims' personal possessions. Falstaff again changes the subject, indicating that he is very melancholy. When Hal makes fun of him, Falstaff sadly regrets that the prince has corrupted him. He remarks that before he knew Hal he was a virtuous man, and that he is determined to reform. Hal immediately offers to join him in stealing a purse, to which Falstaff readily agrees. Hal then asks whether this response suggests any imminent moral reform, but Falstaff asserts that purse-taking is his occupation and it is never a sin "for a man to labor in his vocation."

Ned Poins, an immoral young man and friend of the prince, enters and proposes that they actually do steal a purse that night at Gad's Hill. He has learned of a group of rich citizens travelling to London who will make ready prey. Hal refuses, but Poins assures Falstaff that he can persuade the prince to join them. After Falstaff leaves, Poins proposes that he and Hal only pretend to join in the robbery but really so arrange things that, disguised, they will steal the money from Falstaff and his cohorts rather than from the citizens. Poins suggests the great sport they will have at Falstaff's expense as the old knight tries later to explain what has happened to the money. Hal agrees carelessly, and bids Poins an abrupt farewell.

Hal closes the scene with his most famous speech in the play, in which he explains that his present life is but a device for keeping his future greatness "under wraps," so that when he does become king, the people will be more surprised and impressed than they would be if he were to adhere to all the forms and conventions appropriate to a royal prince.

Commentary

While the first scene introduces the themes to be developed in the historical portions of the play, the second scene introduces the themes important to the comic portions. These themes are stated and restated in varied forms, as is the case in most popular Elizabethan comic action. All Falstaff's flaws are reviewed in Hal's opening speech: his drinking, his overeating, his love of sleep, his fondness for harlots, and his stealing purses from unwary travellers at night. We also are introduced to the mode of dialogue which will predominate in the comic scenes. Plays on words, many indecent, are numerous — some hardly noticeable to a modern audience. The sentences are long, balanced, and subtle — typical of much prose of the period. They are also filled with colloquialisms.

A sentence of Hal's asserting that the life of a highwayman has its ups and downs may serve as an example of these traits:

> As for proof now: a purse of gold most resolutely snatched on Monday night and most dissolutely spent on Tuesday morning; got with swearing 'Lay by,' and spent by crying 'Bring in'; now in as low an ebb as the foot of the ladder, and by-and-by in as high a flow as the ridge of the gallows.
>
> (Act. I, Sc. 2, 31-36)

The sentence is made up of three neatly balanced phrases: (1) "snatched on Monday . . . spent on Tuesday . . .;" (2) "got with swearing . . . and spent by crying . . .;" (3) "now in as low an ebb . . . by-and-by in as high a flow. . . ." Each phrase restates or adds to the former phrase; but the final restatement ironically changes the implication of the whole statement and makes us realize that Hal is defending law and order and satirizing Falstaff's criminal tendencies. The "ups and downs" of the situation, through an implied play on words, literally refer to hanging. The involved nature of the syntax, the unexpected twists that Shakespeare works into it, and the use of colloquial phrases such as "lay by" (or "hands up") may make reading or hearing this kind of prose somewhat tedious today, but its breadth of implication and the richness of its effect ultimately make it as rewarding for theater audiences in our time as is the poetry of the historical scenes.

Finally, Falstaff's basic comic technique — his willingness to twist logic to his own advantage — is revealed in these lines. Falstaff's final response to Hal, " 'Tis no sin for a man to labor in his vocation," is typical of the means by which he gets out of difficult situations throughout this play and its sequel.

The lines up until Poins' departure shed light on his function and character in the play. Poins, the prince's confidant and alter-ego, has little of Falstaff's brilliant, unorthodox wit, but serves chiefly as a second to the prince in stimulating Falstaff's uproarious responses. A knight, young and similar in appearance to the prince (as Falstaff points out in *Henry IV*, Part 2), Poins fulfils an image of decadent nobility less appealing than the stout knight, Falstaff, whom we forgive for his humorous outlook on the world. Poins is not the satirist Falstaff is, but a rebellious late adolescent given to playing practical jokes, whose humor possesses little of the scope and variety of Falstaff's.

Throughout, one gets the feeling that the prince, while spending a great deal of his time in Poins's company, has little respect for him. It is, after all, following Poins' departure that Hal responds, "I know you all, and will a while uphold/ The unyoked humor of your idleness." Falstaff is, of course, included in the prince's "all," but Poins is the figure most immediately in mind at this point.

Hal's speech is his most important one in the play, although it has caused a good deal of disagreement among commentators. Some feel that it shows Hal to be a cold, calculating individual intent on using the warmth and good fellowship of his carefree companions to draw attention to his later, unexpected reformation. Such an interpretation is accurate in part, but it misunderstands the nature of both parts of *Henry IV* as history plays. The speech reveals Hal's understanding of his political image. All his father's known qualities of leadership and his devotion to the highest chivalric ideals have not prevented the rebellion and civil strife which have developed in the kingdom. King Henry has been a man of strength and action throughout his career, yet at the same time he has been predictable, and his enemies have known how and when to attack him, as the following scene will show. Hal, who, as everyone in Shakespeare's audience well knew, was to have a far more successful reign than his father, wishes to remain unknown, unpredictable, and therefore the more wondered at. In his later reign he will always keep his enemies guessing and off-balance. If the play were nothing more than a study in character, the speech might suggest Hal's cold, calculating nature. But as a history play, it rather suggests political ingenuity of a kind probably unknown in medieval England.

Hal's associations with Falstaff and company (his "base contagious clouds") will actually have a beneficial effect on him which he does not here acknowledge. They teach him things about basic human motives and the folly of excessive chivalric honor which he will never learn at court. Statements and actions later in this play and in the later play, *Henry V*, strongly suggest Hal's debt to his tavern companions and the good use he will make of what he has learned from them.

Notes

Hybla: There were several cities in ancient Sicily named Hybla; of these the one on the slope of Mount Etna was mentioned by the ancient Latin poets as being famous for its bees and honey. Shakespeare also refers to the "Hybla bees" in *Julius Caesar*. .

My old lad of the castle: The character Sir John Falstaff was originally given the name Sir John Oldcastle in this play, though his name was changed to its present form before the play was printed for the first time in 1598. "My old lad of the castle" may be a play upon his original name, which was probably changed in deference to the Sir John Oldcastle, who was a well-known person at the time when the play was first acted.

Is not a buff jerkin a most sweet robe of durance? Sheriffs' officers were formerly clad in buff, and the meaning of the prince's question is that it would be delightful to go to prison for getting into debt to their sweet hostess.

For obtaining of suits: When spoken of a person suing in court, this implies a favorable answer *to petitions;* the suit that a hangman obtains is the *clothes* of his victim.

Gib-cat: a tom cat.

Lugged bear: Baited bear. Bear-baiting with dogs was a popular sport.

The melancholy of Moor Ditch: In the *Penniless Pilgrimage* (1618), Taylor speaks of "Moorditch Melancholy" in reference to stagnant water drained into it from the Moorfields. According to Stowe's *Survey,* Moorditch separated Bedlam Hospital for the Insane from the land surrounding it. This would give additional emphasis to its association with melancholy.

Wisdom cries out in the streets. Obviously a reference to Proverbs, Ch. I, v. 20-24 — "Wisdom crieth without; she uttereth her voice in the streets."

Baffle: To degrade. The term originally applied to the form of punishment inflicted on disloyal knights for their infamy; it included hacking their spurs from their heels and suspending them by the heels from a tree.

Cozening: To "cozen" is literally to trick or cheat by imposing on the generosity or hospitality of anyone by a pretence of relationship with him. The meaning of the word has broadened to mean "to trick" or "to cheat" by any method.

Yedward: Edward. The Anglo-Saxon "aed" prefix occurs in many Christian names, e.g., Edgar, Edwin, and denotes happiness or blessedness. The Saxon and early English spelling of Edward would be Aedward or Eadward, which would account for its corruption into Yedward by Shakespeare by reason of its original pronunciation, which was probably still in popular use when this play was written.

If thou darest not stand for ten shillings: A joke on the word "royal," which was a gold piece of the value of ten shillings. See Act II, Sc. 4, 326.

All-hallown summer: The re-appearance of summery weather, which frequently occurs at All-hallows or All Saints' day, the first of November. Like "latter spring" of the previous line, it is used figuratively to denote "thou aged youth," in reference to the boyish nature and foolish pranks which were so unexpectedly encountered in one of the age and habit of Falstaff.

ACT I • SCENE 3

Summary

At court, the king chastises the Earl of Worcester for the lack of respect the Earl — along with his brother Henry Percy, Earl of Northumberland, and his nephew the younger Henry Percy (Hotspur) — have lately been showing the crown. Worcester reminds the king that his succession to the throne was largely achieved through their efforts, for which remark the king immediately banishes Worcester from court. Northumberland speaks next, explaining that his son's reported refusal to turn over prisoners taken in his Scottish victory has been misrepresented to the king. Hotspur speaks next, describing at length the incident involving his refusal. He was visited, in the midst of battle, by a "neat, and trimly dressed" courtier, who wore perfume and used snuff. The man's indifference to the battle at hand so irritated Hotspur that he hardly heard the request for the prisoners and he asks that his answer not be taken as a sign of disloyalty. The king points out, however, that Hotspur still refuses to turn over the prisoners unless Mortimer (Hotspur's brother-in-law) is ransomed, and Mortimer, the king again asserts, is a traitor. Hotspur heatedly denies the charge, saying Mortimer fought bravely and tirelessly with Glendower before being captured. The king denies Hotspur's claim, sternly orders Hotspur to turn over his prisoners, then abruptly leaves the scene.

Following the king's hasty departure, Hotspur goes into a fit of defiant rage, scarcely rational, and all aimed at the king, whom he refers to now by his youthful nickname, Bolingbroke. Worcester and Northumberland seek to quiet him, but the greater their efforts, the more unrestrained his outbreak becomes, particularly when he is informed that King Richard, before his death, had proclaimed Mortimer rightful heir to the throne. Among other things, Hotspur threatens to train a bird to cry nothing but "Mortimer" and give it to the king. Worcester assures him that they will take action which will be "full of peril and adventurous spirit," but Hotspur is lost in private thoughts on the subject of honor:

> By heaven, methinks it were an easy leap,
> To pluck bright honor from the pale-faced moon,
> Or dive into the bottom of the deep,

Where fathom line could never touch the ground,
And pluck up drownèd honor by the locks,
So he that doth redeem her thence might wear
Without corrival all her dignities;
But out upon this half-faced fellowship!
(Act I, Sc. 3, 201-208)

Worcester and Northumberland, observing that Hotspur has become so involved in passionate metaphors that it is almost impossible to understand what he is saying, suggest that they speak with him some other time. After several apologies followed by renewed interruptions, Hotspur agrees to hear Worcester's plan for rebellion, which, he is assured, has many powerful supporters.

Commentary

Introducing Hotspur seems the chief purpose of this scene. Hotspur's well-known description of the elegant courtier visiting him in battle is actually window-dressing as far as the Percies' real motives are concerned. But the speech is a revealing and amazingly convincing image of himself in battle confronting the kind of person he would detest above all: an overdressed, affected dandy. Whatever else Hotspur is, he is honest and unaffected, unable to abide pretence in any form. The attitudes he describes in himself are completely appropriate. He is a plain-spoken, hot-tempered man of action. Despite the vividness of the description, however, the king is quick to observe that Hotspur still refuses to turn over the prisoners, which evokes Hotspur's real objective — the release of his brother-in-law Mortimer.

Whereas the release of Mortimer is probably as far as Hotspur wishes to go, the same cannot be said for Worcester and Northumberland. Having failed to achieve the power they feel is their due for having helped King Henry depose King Richard, they now seek to bring down the man they put upon the throne. Throughout, Hotspur is the tool of his father and uncle, ready to throw himself into rebellion in response to real or imagined insults to his honor, whereas they are simply politicians seeking power.

Even more than the first part of the scene, the conclusion focuses on the changing, self-centered, but utterly unaffected character of Hotspur in contrast to the bemused attitude of his conniving uncle, Worcester, who masterminds the revolt and who is as evasive and tight-lipped as the nephew is direct and outspoken. If the way of life Hotspur stands for is rejected in the play, it is so because it is romantic, no longer practical, not because it lacks any heroic qualities. Hotspur is clearly an attractive, if somewhat comic, figure in the scene. His comic excess is his exaggerated sense of chivalric honor which prevents him from seeing beyond his own injured feelings to the need for national unity. He takes himself too seriously, and the well-being of his country not seriously enough. Thus, he is easy prey for a conniving and self-seeking villain like Worcester, and Worcester desperately needs the warmth and spontaneity Hotspur provides for a successful rebellion.

Notes

I will from henceforth . . . than my condition. "Condition" is used to express "disposition" in the same way that we still speak of a well- or ill-conditioned person. The sense of the passage is that the king will henceforth assume the character that becomes him as a king, mighty and fearful, rather than continue to be cold and moderate in accordance with his natural disposition.

The moody frontier of a servant brow: Frontier, as used by Shakespeare, means generally a fortified earthwork. Here, the frontier of a brow is used metaphorically to denote the forehead on which sullenness and gloom are depicted.

Pouncetbox: A small box used as a receptacle for snuff or scented powder. The lid was usually cut with an open work design.

Took it in snuff: With resentment. Shakespeare puns on the "sniff" which is indicative of anger and the "sniff" when taking snuff.

Parmacity; A corruption of spermaceti: a fatty product from the head of the sperm-whale. It was formerly used chiefly in the composition of ointments.

His brother-in-law, the foolish Mortimer: There is a confusion of persons here. Although in line 142 of this scene, Hotspur terms Mortimer "my wive's brother," and in Act II, Scene 3, 78, Lady Percy speaks of "her brother Mortimer," in Act III, Scene 1, 194, Mortimer himself terms Lady Percy "aunt," and elsewhere terms Hotspur "cousin," which was the true relationship. The confusion arose through both uncle and nephew being named "Edmund Mortimer," Earl of March. The father was Lady Percy's brother; the son, the Mortimer of this play, was her nephew.

Indent with fears: Bargain or covenant with persons who are the object of fears (i.e., those who are our enemies).

Crisp: Curly, wavy. The head of a river is described by Shakespeare as "crisp" in reference to the curls or ripples on the surface of the water. In this connection it is interesting to note that water is depicted in heraldry by means of wavy lines.

Murderous subornation: Incitement to murder, in this case, the murder of Richard II, Henry IV's predecessor on the throne.

Canker: The wild rose or an ulcer.

Send Danger . . . the north to south. Hotspur brags that he does not in the least care what danger he encounters in his pursuit of honor.

Half-faced fellowship: The general meaning is of little worth or contemptible. According to most commentators "half-faced" implies a standing sideways, as for example the profile of a monarch's head on a piece of money; half-faced was thus used to mean anything unsubstantial, thin or miserable. Compare *Henry IV*, Part II, Act III, Scene 2, 283, where Shakespeare refers to a shadow as being "half-faced."

Sword and buckler Prince of Wales: The short sword and buckler (shield) were fighting equipment, not of gentlemen, but of serving-men. Hotspur is insultingly classifying the prince as vulgar, common.

This vile politician: The word politician is here and generally used by Shakespeare in an unfavorable sense as one who pursues a crafty, underhanded policy; a schemer or conspirator. It is hardly ever used by Shakespeare in the modern sense. *Cf. King Lear,* Act VI, Scene 6, 75.

Ravenspurgh: An important town at the mouth of the River Humber which has, since the days of King Henry IV, disappeared owing to the encroachment of the sea. Bolingbroke, afterwards King Henry IV, is supposed to have erected a cross there to celebrate his safe landing with his forces at that place in July, 1399, when he successfully challenged King Richard II for possession of the throne of England.

The Lord Scroop: He was actually cousin to the Archbishop, not brother as given by Shakespeare, and one of the favorites of King Richard II. He fled to Bristol with Bushy, Green, and other accomplices. They were captured by King Henry IV and were summarily executed. Shakespeare, in his play *Richard II*, refers to the death of Bushy and Green, but makes no reference in his works, except the one under discussion, to the death of Lord Scroop.

ACT II • SCENE 1

Summary

Two "carriers" (porters) and "an ostler" (a groom) converse in the yard of the inn which houses the intended victims of the robbery Poins has been planning. The three make vulgar jokes about the sorry state of the inn, including allusions to its thriving insect life and poor sanitary conditions. They are joined by Gadshill, a highwayman. (He is not to be confused with Gad's Hill, the locality which is the setting of the following scene, though he almost certainly takes his name from it.) After a few abusive exchanges, the carriers go out, and Gadshill is joined by the chamberlain, the manager of the inn. Obviously in league with Gadshill, the chamberlain informs him of a landowner staying there for the night who has a large sum of money with him. Gadshill suggests that this landowner is in great danger of being robbed, with which the chamberlain knowingly agrees. Then Gadshill indicates that the thieves he is in league with — that is, of course, Falstaff, Poins, and the prince — are not poor beggars who must steal on foot, but noblemen off on a spree, and that the chamberlain is likely to benefit from his association with Gadshill.

Commentary

This scene's chief function seems to be that of creating a proper atmosphère for the action the prince of Wales is about to be part of. Hal can sink no lower than the world of Gadshill, the chamberlain and the carriers and ostlers. The vulgarity of their jokes, their generally limited and contemptuous view of man, and their infinite corruptibility attest far better to the totally ill-bred, lawless, disorderly life the prince has become part of in his escape from the dark politics of the court than do Jack Falstaff and Ned Poins.

Notes

Out of all cess: Cess was a tax or subsidy, which was levied by regular and moderate rates, so that when anything was exorbitant, or out of measure, it was said to be *out of all cess.*

Stung like a tench: The tench, a fresh-water fish, has red markings which resemble flea bites.

King Christen: Christian king. The Folios read, "King of Christendom."

Turkeys: In spite of their name, which was given to them under a misapprehension as to their origin, turkeys were introduced into this country from America, which was not discovered until nearly a century after King Henry IV began to reign. Thus the mention of turkeys in this play is an *anachronism*.

At hand, quoth pick-purse: A proverbial expression used by many authors of the period; "at hand" signifies that the speaker, here a pick-pocket, is close by and ready.

St. Nicholas' clerks: St. Nicholas was the patron saint of students and scholars; hence the use of the word "clerks". In reality, St. Nicholas is here used for "Old Nick" or the devil, and by his clerks are meant robbers and evil-doers.

Great oneyers: Officers.

Such as can hold in: Variously explained as "such as can curb the law," "such as stick to one another," "such as can keep their own secret."

The receipt of fernseed: Fernseed had the reputation of being able to confer on its possessor the gift of invisibility.

Purchase: A legal term signifying acquisition by any means other than inheritance, including theft.

ACT II • SCENE 2

Summary

Prince Hal and Poins enter near the spot appointed for the robbery. They are followed by Falstaff, whose horse Poins has stolen so that the fat old knight must go on foot. Falstaff hurls a steady stream of abuse at Poins, but the prince only laughs at him and instructs him to put his ear to the ground and listen for the travellers they plan to rob. Falstaff asks whether the prince has any levers to lift him up once he is on the ground, and again demands to know the whereabouts of his horse. The prince replies that he will not be Falstaff's "ostler" (groom). With this, Gadshill indicates that the victims are at hand, and Hal suggests that he and Poins go a bit farther down the road so that if the rest for some reason miss the victims, he and Poins can catch them. Falstaff fears that the travellers may then be too strong for his group, but Hal warns him not to be a coward. After Poins tells Falstaff the whereabouts of his horse, Hal and Poins leave the scene. The travellers are quickly overcome by Falstaff and his followers, but the latter in turn flee because of the unexpected assault by Hal and Poins. The money in hand, Hal and Poins laugh at the image of the frightened Falstaff who "sweats to death and lards the lean earth as he walks along."

Commentary

Little can be said of the robbery scene other than that it is exactly what we expect. The comedy is broad, almost entirely based on Falstaff's bulk and cowardice. The business of the stolen horse and the trick of the second robbery are rooted in the fun and pranks of the medieval English countryside, and are closer in spirit to the earlier anonymous dramatic treatment of story (The *Famous Victories of Henry V*) and to the many legends surrounding Prince Hal and his rowdy companions than anything else in the play. Farce, rather than the subtlety of Falstaff's wit, is the predominant cause of laughter here, and in this respect the scene also has much in common with Shakespeare's later comedy, *The Merry Wives of Windsor*, probably written to take advantage of Falstaff's great popularity. What Falstaff is finally remembered for in *Henry IV* is not the capers of the fat, boastful old knight, but the subtle and penetrating critiques of false values implicit in his various poses and in his comments on the nature of honor. But if Falstaff were nothing more than what he appears to be in this scene, actors through the ages would not have found the role so difficult to play.

Notes

Frets like a gummed velvet: A comparison frequently encountered in the old comedies. Frets has two meanings: 1) fumes or 2) wears away. Velvet was customarily stiffened with gum, and therefore liable to wear.

Four foot by the squire: Four measured feet. *Cf. The Winter's Tale*, Act IV, Scene 4, 349, "jumps twelve foot and a half by the squire."

Sir John Paunch: A fitting nick-name devised for Falstaff. Note the play on the name John of *Gaunt* in the next line.

Now cannot I strike him. Even now I cannot lay hold of him. "Strike" is here probably used in the same sense as in the expression "to strike a path," or "to strike oil."

Happy man be his dole. May everyone have happiness as his share. This phrase is used four times by Shakespeare in his plays (*The Winter's Tale*, Act I, Scene 2, 163; *The Merry Wives of Windsor*, Act III, Scene 4, 68; *The Taming of the Shrew*, Act I, Scene 1, 144; and the present instance). It is probable that it was a catch-phrase current at the time.

Grandjurors: Persons of substance and importance, who alone are summoned to serve on the grand juries at assizes and sessions, in contrast to the common jurors who might not have the qualifications as property holders which render them eligible for service on a grand jury.

ACT II • SCENE 3

Summary

Alone in his castle, Hotspur reads aloud a letter from a lord who declines to take part in the rebellion because he fears the danger of the venture, the uncertainty of the alliances, the poor timing, and the great power of the king. Utterly contemptuous of what he considers to be the man's cowardice, Hotspur vigorously defends the enterprise, pointing out that all life's activities are dangerous, but out of danger comes security. He praises his allies and ends by wishing he had never tried to move "such a dish of skim milk with so honorable an action!" suggesting that the writer of the letter will probably report everything to the king.

Hotspur is joined by his wife, Lady Percy (referred to as Kate), who complains bitterly of Hotspur's recent outward signs of disaffection. He has banished her from his bed for over two weeks, and goes about obviously preoccupied with thoughts and imaginings associated with battle. Hotspur ignores her, and in response to her asking him what "carries [him] away" (distracts him), Hotspur answers: "Why, my horse, my love, my horse." He continues to banter with her in this manner until Lady Percy loses her temper and threatens to break Hotspur's little finger if he does not tell her what is going on. Hotspur abruptly dismisses her, saying that he will have nothing to do with love and women, and calls for his horse. She asks him if he loves her. He answers that when he is on horseback, then he will swear he loves her "infinitely." She must not, he says, ask him where he is going. He also remarks that he can trust her with secret information as far as he can trust any woman; that is, not at all. But, he adds, her curiosity will be satisfied in that she is to follow him to his secret destination the next day.

Commentary

Hotspur's reaction to the letter he reads is completely in keeping with the Hotspur spirit. Hotspur is both star of the team and captain of the cheering section. Nothing offends him so much as the overly cautious man, one who "looks before he leaps." This correspondent may be the "dish of skim milk" Hotspur says he is, but it is worth noting that, as the play reveals, his fears are well-founded. The king's force ultimately does prove too strong, and Hotspur's allies, including his own father, fail to supply their support at the crucial moment. But a cause involving his honor is like an addiction with Hotspur. He must pursue it, heart and soul, without weighing possible consequences.

The most striking thing about this scene is its comedy. To be sure, this act is dominated by the comic, but it is surprising to see Hotspur in this vein. The fact is, of course, that this is comedy of a quite different kind from that instigated by Falstaff, and this scene, paired with the one following it, provides one aspect of the play's chief contrast. Even in a comic situation, Hotspur is fundamentally a man of passion. Hotspur's attitude towards his wife in this scene is quite gruff, but not at all cold. There is little doubt that he and his wife are in love and understand each other very well. Lady Percy is a perfect mate for him. His teasing represents an exaggeration of traditional male disdain for woman; hers an equally comic exaggeration of feminine curiosity and sudden changes of mood. Both play their roles to the hilt, not satirically, but fully aware of what they are, and richly enjoying it. His soldierly claim that he will swear his love only when he is on horseback seems a caricature of the famous lines of the lover in Lovelace's *To Lucasta* (written quite a few years later): "I could not love thee dear so much, Loved I not Honor more." But Hotspur treats the theme with a rough abandon quite foreign to Lovelace's courtly figure, and it is this quality, combined with the incredible vitality in the reactions of both Hotspur and his wife, that makes these figures so attractive at the same time that they approach caricature. The scene seems placed at this point in the play to stress the difference, in an informal, if not comic, situation, between the old tradition — emotional, courageous, and single-minded, — and the new, cynical, compromising spirit represented in the scenes involving Falstaff and the prince. The contrast will shortly be made explicit by Hal himself.

Notes

My lord of York: Richard Scroop, Archbishop of York. See Act I, Scene 3, 268.

How now, Kate: The name of Hotspur's wife was really Elizabeth. She was sister to Mortimer, Earl of March, and aunt to Edmund Mortimer.

Esperance: The motto and war-cry of the Percy family. It means hope.

Mammets: A word derived from the old French *Mahomet*, an idol, from the mistaken notion that Mohammedans were worshippers of idols. The signification in the present instance is "dolls" or "puppets."

ACT II • SCENE 4

Summary

Prince Hal, awaiting Falstaff at the Tavern in Eastcheap, has been entertaining himself by drinking and joking with the tapsters, whom he, oddly as the Prince of Wales, calls by their first names and to whom he feels himself "sworn brother." He comments on their use of colloquialisms and their gullibility, proposing to Poins that they while away the time until Falstaff's arrival by having fun at the expense of Francis, one of the most naïve of the serving boys. From the next room, Poins demands Francis' services, while the prince questions him on a variety of matters, thus preventing the boy from doing his job. The trick achieves its intended effect of thoroughly confusing the poor boy, whose woes are added to by the vintner (wine merchant), who impatiently asks why Francis does not respond to Poins' demands. The prince is thoroughly delighted with the proceedings, and when everyone else leaves the stage, he reflects happily on the fact that he is "not yet of Percy's mind, the Hotspur of the North; he that kills . . . some six or seven dozen of Scots at a breakfast, washes his hands, and says to his wife, 'Fie upon this quiet life! I want work.' " Hal goes on to lampoon Lady Percy's reaction — " 'O my sweet Harry,' says she, 'how many hast thou killed today?' " — and calls for Falstaff to join him in acting out the scene.

Jack Falstaff enters, calling for sack and ranting oaths against all cowards — by whom he presumably means Hal and Poins, who failed to aid Falstaff and his followers in their hour of need. Falstaff's melancholy leads him to conclude that all things in the world have been corrupted. There is no manhood left, and, worse still, even the wine he drinks tastes impure. Pretending not to understand what Falstaff is grumbling about, Hal asks what is the matter. Falstaff inquires whether he and Poins are not cowards, at which Hal pretends to become angry and threatens violence. Falstaff then describes the theft followed by the attack by unknown assailants who made off with the loot, and asks why Hal and Poins did not help him. Hal suggests that he describe in detail what happened. Falstaff maintains that he and his followers were attacked by a hundred men and that he himself held off a dozen of them for two hours. He shows as evidence holes in his clothing and his hacked sword. Falstaff later reduces the number he fought with to fifty, and sadly acknowledges that he was forced to kill two of them. But this number grows. Next it becomes four that Falstaff killed, then seven, nine, and finally eleven. Falstaff's exciting but thoroughly blurred description of his combat is interrupted by comments by Hal and Poins, most of them playing on words Falstaff has used and mocking the obvious lies Falstaff is telling. Having reached eleven, Falstaff tells how three "knaves" dressed in green came at him from behind and attacked him unseen, since it was so dark one could not see his own hand. After an outburst of insult and abuse, Hal asks how Falstaff could have known the knaves were dressed in green if it was as dark as Falstaff says. Caught, Falstaff refuses to answer, and apparently Hal and Poins draw their swords, because, assuming a pose of injured pride, Falstaff insists he will say nothing under compulsion. After another volley of exchanged insults, Hal tells him precisely what happened, that after the four in Falstaff's group robbed the four travellers, they were in turn attacked by two — Hal and Poins — who have the money to prove it. Poins asks Falstaff how he proposes to get around these facts. Falstaff explains. Was it for him, he asks, "to kill the heir apparent?" He knew instinctively that his assailant was the Prince of Wales and therefore was "a coward on instinct." But, he says, rapidly changing the subject, he is glad they have the money, suggests they immediately begin to make merry, and proposes they have "a play extempore," a charade or brief spontaneous play frequently performed by groups in taverns to entertain themselves. Hal agrees and suggests that the subject be Falstaff's "running away," but Falstaff pleads that there be "no more of that."

The hostess enters with news that a messenger has come from the king, but with Hal's permission, Falstaff goes out to dismiss the messenger. During Falstaff's absence, Hal asks Peto and Bardolph their role in Falstaff's charade. They confess to having bloodied their garments and hacked their swords to lend credibility to his story. After a lively conversation focusing on Bardolph's known reputation as a thief and the redness of his nose, they are once again joined by Falstaff, who is memorably hailed by Hal:

> Here comes lean Jack; here comes barebone. How now, my sweet creature of bombast [cotton batting]? How long is't ago, Jack, since thou sawest thine own knee?
>
> (Act II, Sc. 4, 310-312)

Falstaff claims that he was once "an eagle's talon in the waist," but that he has swelled up with "sighing and grief." He informs Hal that the king has summoned him to court because of the uprising by Hotspur, Douglas, and the wild Welsh fellow whose name Falstaff cannot remember. Hal reminds him of the name, Owen Glendower, which sets off a series of jokes directed at that Welshman's boastfulness. Falstaff suggests that Hal "practice an answer" for his forthcoming interview with his father. Hal proposes that they act out the interview, with Falstaff playing the role of the king. The hostess squeals with delight as Falstaff assumes his throne (a joint-stool) and royal accessories (a dagger for scepter and a pillow for crown). In his imperial role, Falstaff chastises Hal for his bad companions and way of life, but acknowledges that there is an admirable man in Hal's company named Falstaff. Banish the rest, he advises, but keep Falstaff. This is too much for Hal, who suggests they reverse roles. Pretending to feel irritation that he is being "deposed," Falstaff agrees. Hal, now as the king, immediately plunges into a condemnation of the "devil" who haunts Hal "in the likeness of an old fat man." The speech is a masterpiece of insult:

> Why dost thou converse with that trunk of humors, that bolting hutch of beastliness, that swoll'n parcel of dropsies, that huge bombard of sack, that stuffed cloakbag of guts, that roasted Manningtree ox with the pudding in his belly, that reverend vice, that grey iniquity, that father ruffian, that vanity in years? Wherein is he good, but to taste sack and drink it? wherein neat and cleanly, but to carve a capon and eat it? wherein cunning, but in craft? wherein crafty, but in villainy? wherein villainous, but in all things? wherein worthy, but in nothing? (Act II, Sc. 4, 426-436)

Falstaff (as Hal) wonders whom the king has in mind, and finding out that the name is Falstaff, his response and Hal's rejoinder are equally memorable:

> But to say I know more harm in him than in myself were to say more than I know. That he is old, the more the pity, his white hairs do witness it; but that he is (saving your reverence) a whoremaster, that I utterly deny. If sack and sugar be a fault, God help the wicked! If to be old and merry be a sin, then many an old host that I know is damned. If to be fat be to be hated, then Pharaoh's lean kine are to be loved. No, my good lord: banish Peto, banish Bardolph, banish Poins; but for sweet Jack Falstaff, kind Jack Falstaff, true Jack Falstaff, valiant Jack Falstaff, and therefore more valiant, being, as he is, old Jack Falstaff, banish not him thy Harry's company, banish not him thy Harry's company. Banish plump Jack, and banish all the world. (Act II, Sc. 4, 442-456)

Bardolph interrupts this "play extempore" with word that the sheriff and his "watch" (posse) are at the door looking for those who committed the robbery. Hal advises Falstaff to hide behind a curtain while he throws the sheriff off the track. The sheriff enters, claiming that suspects have been traced to the tavern, one of them "well known . . . , / A gross fat man." The prince assures him that the man he describes is not on the premises, but that he, the prince, will see to it that Falstaff reports to the sheriff the next day. After the pacified sheriff leaves, Falstaff is discovered in deep slumber behind the curtain. Hal picks the old knight's pocket, where he finds a bill, undoubtedly from the tavern, listing what Falstaff owes for food and drink. The prince is highly amused to discover that Falstaff has purchased two gallons of sack and only a "half penny-worth" of bread. Hal keeps the bill and tells the group he plans to go to the court in the morning. He also indicates that the stolen money will be returned, and that he will get the "fat rogue" Falstaff a commission in charge of foot soldiers so that he may walk to battle.

Commentary

That Hal is very drunk from the beginning of this whole scene until near the end of it is important to bear in mind. In a way, he resembles the rather careless, almost surly Hotspur of the previous scene. The difference lies in the source of their drunkenness. Whereas Hotspur could literally be called "drunk with honor" — so single-minded in devotion to his own ego that he is practically indifferent to everything and everyone else — Hal's state results strictly from an excess of ale. The description of his conversation with the tapsters and the trick he and Poins play on the unfortunate Francis suggest an image of Hal at his most irresponsible. Nowhere is the life he will one day "throw off" so vividly represented. Yet like drunkenness itself, Hal in fact can throw this life off; Hotspur never can his. Hotspur's illusions constitute a drunkenness from which he can never recover. Hal finally makes explicit the distinction between his excess and Hotspur's and indicates that no matter if he is drunk and acting foolishly with foolish companions, he still does not approach the foolishness of Hotspur's mania for personal honor. That Hal's exaggeration of a conversation between Hotspur and his wife is not too far from the truth is strongly indicated by the juxtaposition of this scene with the last. Hotspur's attitudes invite parody; Hal, and later Falstaff, perform the task with great skill. Hal's call for Falstaff to act out with him the dialogue between Hotspur and wife leads into the dominant action of the scene, though the charade they finally do perform parodies figures closer to Hal than Hotspur. Hal's call here for Falstaff is significant, however, since it foreshadows the satirical climax of the scene.

After taking note of the brilliant and incredibly subtle quality of the comedy in this scene, one questions, inevitably, just how big an act Falstaff is putting on. Obviously, he tells the story of his epic struggle following the robbery more to entertain the prince than to mask the truth from him, and just as obviously he shifts his ground with great gusto when informed who his unknown attackers were. But it is just as possible that Falstaff knows from the start who attacked him and uses the whole occasion to fabricate a magnificent charade. There is nothing in Falstaff's lines to indicate how much in control of the situation he is, but such a trick would be completely in character. Whether he knows the identity of his assailants or not, he certainly is aware of the performance he is giving, and reveals his mastery of the form of entertainment he has selected — subtle, infinitely flexible mimicry and parody. Rarely when Falstaff is on stage does he not mimic some tradition, concept, or person. His first pose in this episode — and his most common one throughout the play — is that of the righteous person scandalized at the sorry condition of man and the world. "Good manhood" has disappeared and it is time for the likes of "old Jack" to pass on. Certainly there is no attempt to mask hypocrisy here. The lines may in fact be intended to parody Hotspur's observations on cowardice in the previous scene. Falstaff's pose shifts with lightning speed. Next he is the fearless knight describing and acting out his battle experiences for a group of fascinated admirers, allowing the number of his victims to grow as his narrative progresses. Hal and Poins punctuate his performance with sarcastic and irreverent remarks, however, which makes the role Falstaff assumes here the more ridiculous. One cannot help feeling that Falstaff wants to appear as ridiculous as possible — even in his efforts to get confirmation of his feats from Bardolph and Gadshill. Faced with Hal's and Poins' swords and their precise statement of the circumstances surrounding the robbery, Falstaff assumes his most obvious and ridiculous role of all — that of the subject so instinctively sensitive to the inner qualities of royalty that he could not do harm to his prince, even when he did not know that he was the prince.

In order to change the subject as quickly as possible, Falstaff proposes that they act out a brief, spontaneous play, which they indeed shortly perform; but the fact is, the whole episode has been a "play extempore" in which the central figure has been Falstaff, with Hal and Poins feeding him lines. Since Falstaff himself does not believe in the sacredness of tradition, he views tradition and its effects on human behavior in terms of comic theater in which he is creator, director, and chief actor. His overall success in this venture is attested to by his unparalleled popularity with audiences throughout the world for over four hundred and fifty years.

It is hard to find comic dialogue in Shakespeare to match Falstaff's in variety, broad humor, quickness of wit, and relevance to the overall meaning of the play. The "play extempore," in particular, must be seen, or at least read aloud, to be fully appreciated. Falstaff continues to pass from one pose to another, richly enjoying the inconsistency. Perhaps the most common of his poses is that of the suffering and pious man, here uproariously given as the reason for his great bulk — "A plague a sighing and grief, it blows a man up like a bladder." He next assumes a degree of pomposity in forgetting the name of an extremely pompous person, Owen Glendower. But the monumental poses of the scene are those in which he parodies the imperial manner (significantly quite unlike the manner of Henry IV himself) and the defender of the innocent against injustice in his eulogy of "sweet Jack Falstaff." His verbal outpouring in the role of virtuous monarch giving advice to his son is in the artificial courtly style of John Lyly's famous prose romance *Euphues* (the style thereby called *euphuistic*). It is characterized by general wordiness, long, balanced sentences, extended similes, quotations from ancient authorities, and rhetorical questions. Falstaff's treatment of the style exaggerates these characteristics and intentionally makes the overall effect almost unbearably tedious. Most writers of prose fiction in the period used the style extensively, and Falstaff's speech satirizes contemporary popular romances and earlier plays more than it satirizes royal pomposity. Falstaff's speech, of course, could imply satire of Henry IV; yet Falstaff avoids any sense of personal satire. He wishes to poke fun at the artificiality and conventionalism of courtly attitudes, not at the man who is Hal's father and king of England. The closest Falstaff comes to playing Henry himself, in fact, is when Hal proposes they change roles and Falstaff asks if Hal would "depose" him, an unmistakable if jesting allusion to the circumstances by which Henry achieved his throne. Since nothing is viewed as sacred in this scene, so disrespectful an allusion can get by. It certainly could not pass unnoticed outside the tavern in Eastcheap, though.

The change of roles in no way shifts the emphasis away from Falstaff. Hal remains the straight man, despite the elaborate abuse he heaps upon Falstaff. Our interest is focused on how Falstaff is going to respond, as it was when he was faced with the indisputable evidence of his lies. The response is one of apparent innocence: "I would your grace would take me with you. Whom means your grace?" Falstaff's response combines in compact form all the variety of his never fully-fathomed humor. At no point do we believe a word he says, yet at no point do we feel anything but love for an old man in whom intelligence and simplicity underlie the hypocrisy and boastfulness that surround him like his great bulk.

Hal's suddenly sober and reflective response ("I do, I will") recalls the overriding theme that the life of the tavern is to be short-lived, that one day it will all be different.

This final episode serves as a kind of supplement to what is surely one of the longest scenes in a Shakespearean play. Following the rich and varied implications of the father-son charade, the action at the end turns back to the less complicated farce of the scene's earlier portions. Falstaff may or may not be "playing" the fat clown asleep behind the tapestry, but either way the effect is to produce laughter, and little else. His overall attitude to both the law and its potential threat to him is summed up by the rapidity with which he falls asleep (or pretends to) while Hal diverts the sheriff.

Notes

Sworn brother: In the days of chivalry there existed among companions in arms a custom of banding themselves together as "sworn brothers" or *fratres jurati*, as they were called. They entered into an oath to share equally in all their undertakings.

Leash of drawers: A "drawer" was a tapster or waiter in an inn. "Leash" is a term borrowed from the sport of hunting, and meant three greyhounds yoked together by one leash or thong.

Corinthian: An expression, current in the time of Shakespeare, and much later, for a young man fond of high living and revelry.

Score a pint of bastard in the Half-moon: "Half-moon" and "Pomgarnet" (i.e., Pomegranate) were names of rooms in the Boar's-Head Tavern, Eastcheap, where this scene is laid. "To score a pint of bastard in the Half-moon" means to put a pint of Spanish wine to the account of the guest in the Half-moon room.

Not-pated: Hair cut short. It was probably the custom only among the upper classes at this time to wear their hair long.

Puke-stocking: "Puke" probably meant dark-colored or woollen.

Caddis-garter: It was customary to wear garters outside the clothing. A caddis-garter would be a garter of worsted or cheap woollen fabric, which would not bear comparison with the fine silken garters worn by fashionable persons.

Spanish-pouch: Variously explained as a fat-bellied man, a human barrel of Spanish wine (and so a tippler), or as the purse or pouch into which the tavern-keeper put his takings.

Rivo: Appears frequently in writers contemporary with Shakespeare as an exclamation used by revellers, but its meaning and origin are unknown.

Titan . . . (pitiful-hearted Titan): Titan is Hyperion the Sun-god. It was the butter that melted, and not the sun-god as Shakespeare's arrangement of the sentence might suggest. Falstaff might from his fatness be compared with "that compound" (i.e., melted butter).

I would I were a weaver. During the persecutions of the Protestants in Flanders under Philip II, those who took refuge in England brought with them the woollen manufacture. These were Calvinists, who were always distinguished by their love of psalmody.

Their points being broken. . . . Note the play on the word "points" which means the sharp end of a sword, and also the lace or string that supports a garment.

In Kendal green: Kendal, a town in Westmoreland, was famous for making and dyeing cloth. "Kendal green" was the livery of Robert, Earl of Huntingdon and his followers while they remained outlaws, and their leader assumed the name of Robin Hood.

Tallow-catch: A receptacle for catching the tallow which drips from a lighted candle. *Tallow-ketch* and *Tallow-keech* have been suggested as emendations, the former signifying a tallow-tub or barrel and the latter a quantity of tallow or fat rolled into a lump.

Strappado: A form of torture, which consisted in raising the victim by his arms, which were tied behind his back, and suddenly letting him drop, so that his arms were wrenched from their sockets.

Royal man: A noble was a coin worth just over 6 shillings; a "royal" was 10 shillings. The hostess was to convert the "nobleman" into a "royal man."

Taken with the manner: "Manner" is an old law term signifying the goods which a thief takes away. The expression "taken with the manner" means "caught in the act."

Thou had'st fire and sword . . . A humorous reference to the fiery color in Bardolph's face. In *King Henry V*, Fluellen describes Bardolph to the King: "one, Bardolph, if your majesty know the man: his face is all bubukles, and whelks, and knobs, and flames o'fire." (Act III, Sc. 6, 108.)

"**These meteors**" and "**exhalations**": "knobs, and flames o'fire" on Bardolph's face.

Portend: Meteors and exhalations were regarded as omens of evil.

Choler, my lord, if rightly taken. A play on words, between "choler" and "collar," and between the meanings of "taken." "My irascible temper, if rightly taken" (i.e., rightly considered), says Bardolph. "No," says the Prince, "if rightly taken" (i.e., if you get your deserts, the "halter," or the hangman's noose.)

Any alderman's thumb-ring: It was the usual custom among persons of importance to wear a ring on the thumb. In the "Squire's Tale" in Chaucer's *Canterbury Tales*, it is said of the rider of the brazen horse who advanced into the hall of Cambuscan that "upon his thumb he had of gold a ring."

Gave Amamon the bastinado: Amamon is the name of some devil or fiend. *Cf. The Merry Wives of Windsor*, Act II, Sc. 2, 311: "Amamon sounds well; Lucifer well; Barbason well; yet they are devils' additions, the names of fiends." *To give the bastinado* means to beat on the soles of the feet.

Welsh hook: Seems to have been a pike with a sharp point and a hook in the place of the ax which was usual in a battle-ax.

In King Cambyses' vein: In an old tragedy by Thomas Preston, *Cambyses, King of Persia* (1570), there is a stage direction: *At this tale told, let the queen weep,* which explains the nature of Cambyses' vein (weeping, emotional tragedy), and also the allusion to "weeping" and "the tristful queen" a few lines later.

Tickle-brain: Appears to have been the nick-name for some kind of strong liquor, and so was suitable to be applied to the hostess of a tavern.

Bombard: A huge leather jar, resembling in shape a "bombard" or cannon used by an attacking force to batter down the walls of a town.

Manningtree ox: This is a huge prime beef ox raised in the pastures of Essex near Manningtree.

That reverend vice: Vice was the chief comic character of the old morality plays: *Iniquity, Ruffian,* and *Vanity* were other characters in these plays.

I deny your major: I deny your major premise. In logic, a syllogism consists of a *major premise,* a *minor premise* and a *conclusion.* In the present instance, major seems to be used in the general sense of "proposition."

A hue and cry: When a felony was committed, it was the practice for the men of the neighborhood to pursue the felon with shouts and horns, and such pursuit and those engaged in it were termed a "hue and cry."

ACT III • SCENE 1

Summary

Hotspur and his allies in rebellion meet at the castle of the Welsh chieftain, Owen Glendower. The controversial Mortimer, now married to Glendower's daughter, states his confidence in the success of the enterprise, but Hotspur, focusing more on immediate practicalities, insists that they discuss how the land is to be divided following their victory. Glendower produces a map and predicts how terrified "Lancaster" (King Henry) will be at the prospect of meeting Hotspur in battle. But then Glendower proceeds to expand upon his own terrifying nature, foretold he says, by fearful omens and strange occurrences which accompanied his birth. Hotspur makes light of Glendower's boasting, and the two begin to argue over the truth of Glendower's mystical powers. Caught up in his rage and frustration over Hotspur's skepticism, Glendower finally shouts that he can "call spirits from the vasty deep," to which Hotspur makes the maddening reply:

> Why, so can I, or so can any man;
> But will they come when you do call for them?
>
> (Act III, Sc.1, 54-55)

Hotspur warns the astounded "magician" to tell the truth. Mortimer begs them to stop quarrelling and discuss division of the kingdom, which they finally agree to do. But that discussion brings renewed combat. Hotspur finds that the proposed geographical division leaves him with less land than the others, and he attempts to alter the map, but Glendower will not "have it altered." Hotspur threateningly tells him to state his opposition in Welsh, but Glendower, misunderstanding the spirit of Hotspur's statement, insists that he speaks English as well as Hotspur, that he was even trained in writing English verse. Hotspur says that he cannot stand verse, that he would rather hear "a dry wheel grate on the axletree. . . ." Finally they agree to leave the map as it is, Hotspur protesting that he really doesn't care, that he would give "thrice so much land" to a "deserving friend," but if bargaining is called for he will quibble over "the ninth part of a hair." Glendower goes out to get their wives so that they may bid them farewell, and Mortimer asks Hotspur why he seems so intent on angering the old man. Hotspur says he cannot help himself, that all Glendower's claims to occult knowledge and mystical power strike him as nonsense. Both Mortimer and Worcester find fault with Hotspur, saying that few men would thus have crossed the renowned Owen Glendower, and that Hotspur's impatience, while it may serve him well in battle, does him little good in political situations.

Glendower returns with the ladies, and explains to Mortimer, whose wife understands no more English than he does Welsh, that Lady Mortimer is deeply distressed about his going off to war. Mortimer speaks tenderly to her, reassuring her of his love. Through Glendower she bids him lie down with his head on her lap so that she may sing to him. Hotspur breaks in, instructing his wife to allow him to do the same, but is quickly hushed. Following the song, Hotspur breaks in again, commenting briefly on its beauty. A sharp exchange with Lady Percy follows, and as Lady Mortimer continues her song, Hotspur insists that his wife also sing a song. Lady Percy refuses, using the oath "in good sooth" in her protest. This provokes a fierce attack by Hotspur on his wife for using an oath appropriate to a citizen's wife. She should, he says, use language, even in swearing, appropriate to the nobility. With this, he goes out abruptly to prepare for their departure to the wars. Mortimer, far more reluctantly, also agrees to leave.

Commentary

There is little doubt that Hotspur gets the better of Glendower in this scene. He sees through the aura of mystery and wonder with which the eminently theatrical Glendower has surrounded himself, and reduces the old sorcerer to size. The treatment of Owen Glendower as essentially a comic figure may well represent Shakespeare's own dismissal of a time honored set of Welsh legends. Glendower had become in the fifteenth and sixteenth centuries something of a symbol of Welsh desire for independence and opposition to the English crown. His actual successes against Henry IV, were little short of phenomenal, largely because of his acute understanding of the uses of guerrilla warfare. Not until Prince Henry (Hal) assumed full control of the forces opposing him was the historical Glendower finally subdued. Later legends picture him still alive in the hills of Wales, planning through sorcery the ultimate freeing of Wales from English domination. Hotspur, then, represents and defends English national pride and chauvinism in ridiculing the Welsh, symbolized by Owen Glendower.

But chauvinistic satire of the mysticism and ambition of the Welsh is only a minor objective in the scene. Its chief function, obviously, has to do with Hotspur, and is a further development of what has already been said about him and his role in the play as a whole. The tough, hard-boiled realist Hotspur is actually as guilty of treason as Glendower, and is, in his glorification of personal honor, as much a victim of his own egocentric illusions. Not only does the scene present a group of power-seeking men dividing up the precious soil of England (an unthinkable crime in the mind of an Elizabethan Englishman), but one of the men is Hotspur, "sweet fortune's minion and her pride" (Act I, Sc. 1, 83). Rebellion leading to deposition is bad enough. But since even Henry IV was guilty on those grounds, might not so noble a figure as Hotspur be forgiven? (Worcester is later to feel that he would indeed be forgiven.) Permanent division of the land is something else, however. Nothing could more quickly disturb the roots of any Englishman than that, and to see Hotspur, with all his honor, participating in such an attempt utterly debases him and reveals that his outdated sense of chivalric honor has led him to as shocking a display of egocentricity as that of his foolish opposite, Glendower. Ironically, Glendower's outward attitudes parallel what is going on inside of Hotspur, despite their heated differences. Hotspur the realist cannot see that he is the victim of illusions about himself that are hardly distinguishable from those he finds so irritating in the old magician.

If the first portion of this scene did not make explicit enough the distorted attitudes Hotspur's exaggerated honor has led him to, the last portion does. Again he plays the bitter realist, with Glendower weaving the magical spells. But this time, since the theme is the beauty and warmth of young love, Glendower is appealing and persuasive, while

Hotspur seems the fool. Glendower must be his daughter's spokesman, while she expresses her feelings, echoing his statements, with her singing. The very qualities in Glendower which produced the earlier boastfulness and bluster now produce rich, sensuous Elizabethan love-verse.

> She bids you on the wanton rushes lay you down
> And rest your gentle head upon her lap,
> And she will sing the song that pleaseth you
> And on your eyelids crown the god of sleep,
> Charming your blood with pleasing heaviness,
> Making such difference 'twixt wake and sleep
> As is the difference betwixt day and night
> The hour before the heavenly-harnessed team
> Begins his golden progress in the east.
>
> (Act III, Sc. 1, 211-219)

Hotspur, whose earlier contempt for poetry effectively put down the pompous Glendower, here breaks into the sweet harmony of the dialogue and makes himself generally obnoxious. The reason for the change is obviously the presence of the ladies, evoking a tone of genuine tenderness and sadness at the imminent separation. Hotspur is so consumed by the fire of his own ego that he is not in the least affected by the sincere and tender sentiments expressed. In making uncouth and insulting remarks to his wife throughout the proceedings, he reveals that he is as far from reality in his thinking as he earlier accused Glendower of being. This situation does not call for his crude soldierly manner, but he is too blind to recognize the fact.

Notes

Burning cressets: A cresset was an open iron-work basket in which fuel was burned to form a beacon or to give light.

Our threefold order ta'en: The division into three parts, upon which they are agreed. That is, the agreement to which Mortimer, Glendower, and Hotspur are parties.

Being sealed interchangeably: There would be three copies of the agreement, each copy being signed by each of the parties.

My father Glendower: Remember that Mortimer had married Glendower's daughter.

Merlin: The famous soothsayer and magician who appears in the legends surrounding King Arthur and his Knights of the Round Table.

Bountiful/As mines of India: To Shakespeare's audiences the vast wealth of India would be proverbial from the exaggerated tales of travellers who had visited such a distant land.

My aunt Percy: Shakespeare here rightly makes Lady Percy the aunt of Mortimer, and not his sister as elsewhere.

The wanton rushes: The usual floor-covering of these times would be rushes spread in abundance.

'Tis a woman's fault. Hotspur seems to mean that he is behaving like woman, who never does what she is wished to do.

Such sarcenet surety: Sarcenet was the name of a very thin filmy silk material which received its name from the Saracens, from which nation it was probably introduced. A "sarcenet surety" would be an infirm or weak security.

Finsbury: The open places and fields at Finsbury, just outside Moorgate, were used by the citizens of London for the practice of archery.

Velvetguards: The wives of the citizens dressed up in their Sunday finery. Velvetguards were the velvet trimmings upon their costumes.

'Tis the next way to turn tailor or be redbreast-teacher. Singing is the nearest or surest way to become a tailor (teacher of singing) to robin redbreast. Hotspur is contemptuous of music and what it leads to.

ACT III • SCENE 2

Summary

Prince Hal arrives at the palace for his confrontation with the king. The latter sends his followers out and scolds Hal severely for his way of life and low companions, again asserting that Hal's behavior must be his own punishment for his misdeeds. Hal admits his guilt but claims that rumor-mongers have exaggerated his sins far beyond their reality. The king launches into an extended speech in which he compares Hal to the irresponsible, pleasure-seeking, spendthrift, young King Richard II, who made his presence in public so common an occurrence that his subjects were never impressed when they saw him. He, Bolingbroke, on the other hand, made sure he was seldom in public view, so that his infrequent appearances would be more "wondered at:"

That men would tell their children, 'This is he!'
Others would say, 'Where, which is Bolingbroke?'
(Act III, Sc. 2, 48-49)

The people, the king says, became so "surfeited" with Richard and his corrupt favorites and base companions that they began to have contempt for him, and the same is now becoming the case with Hal. Though Hal promises to reform, the king presses on with increasing heat. He praises Hotspur, comparing him to himself as the determined young Bolingbroke, and tells of the many powerful lords who are supporting the new rebellion. But he asks why he should say these things to Hal, who may well join the rebels and become Hotspur's follower. Hal, deeply hurt and angered, claims that he will make up for his deficiencies and also surprise his slanderers by one day facing Hotspur in single combat:

And that shall be the day, whene'er it lights,
That this same child of honor and renown,
This gallant Hotspur, this all-praisèd knight,
And your unthought-of Harry chance to meet.
For every honor sitting on his helm,
Would they were multitudes, and on my head
My shames redoubled! For the time will come
That I shall make this northern youth exchange
His glorious deeds for my indignities.
(Act III, Sc. 3, 138-146)

The king, much encouraged, assures Hal of his renewed confidence. Sir Walter Blunt enters and tells them the rebels are assembling at Shrewsbury, and that if all who have pledged them support appear, they will constitute as large a force as ever rose up against the state. The king orders that each of his followers set off as quickly as possible, as he himself will.

Commentary

The confrontation between father and son takes place pretty much as predicted. While the form of Falstaff's parody in Act II, Sc. 2, is not followed, the content is not far off, as it concerns Hal's base companions. Falstaff's image of the king was, of course, based on a highly stylized stage image of royalty in plays of the 1570's and 80's. Shakespeare's king is a good deal beyond that, but Henry here thinks and speaks in conventional terms without looking beneath the surface of things. Henry compares Hal to Richard II, and on the surface the comparison is valid. Richard did, and Hal does, seek physical pleasures with base companions in a spendthrift manner. But there are three all-important differences that Henry does not consider. First, Richard was king when he did these things, and Hal is not. To be king is to have full responsibility in the state; to be heir apparent, as others have observed, is to have none. It is a tedious period of waiting accompanied by the necessity to subordinate one's individuality so as not to embarrass "the establishment" or in some way challenge the *status quo,* of which one is supposed to be an integral part. An energetic, creative, imaginative youth would find it difficult to survive such self-regimentation. That Richard would not discipline himself as king was a deep flaw in his character; that Hal will not as prince is an insignificant one, if it is a flaw at all. Second, Hal has no reason to be a Bolingbroke, even if he wanted to be exactly like his father. Bolingbroke could excel because of the defects of Richard's reign; Hal can hardly excel because of the defects of Henry's. For Hal to be a "chip off the old block" could only result in a rebellious Hal, not a subservient one, and this is clearly not what the king seeks.

The third and most important difference is in the nature of the base companions. The attention given Ned Poins in this play is significant in that the immoral Poins pretty closely parallels King Richard's favorites. Yet Poins is clearly not the companion who holds the central place in Hal's affections. Richard had no Falstaff about him. He might have been better off if he had. Beyond all the tomfoolery and shenanigans, Falstaff's ultimate influence on Hal has to do with common sense, the ability to see and deal with what is genuinely important to one's life and career, and to eliminate the rest. It involves the all-important political reality of compromise, combined with alertness and intelligence. Richard would compromise but he was not alert; Hotspur is alert but he will not compromise. Henry, somewhat more successful politically than both, perhaps lacks some of his son's intelligence. At all events, whatever it is that will make Hal great as king in part derives from what he learns from the immensely quick-witted Falstaff. Thus Falstaff can hardly be considered an utterly unworthy companion.

That Hal is ready to go beyond Falstaff, however, is suggested by his response to his father. He does have a sense of personal honor, and it is deeply offended by what his father has said. His response is as dignified and restrained as Hotspur's earlier response to the king's insults was irrepressible and outlandish. Hal's honor is what it should be, no more and no less:

> I will redeem all this on Percy's head
> And, in the closing of some glorious day,
> Be bold to tell you that I am your son, . . .
>
> (Act III, Sc. 3, 132-134)

In all respects, Hal can and will bide his time, which can be said for no one else in the play. And while he bides his time, he is fulfilling the essential duty of Prince of Wales. He is learning to be a good king.

Notes

I stole all courtesy from heaven . . . An allusion to the classical myth of Prometheus, who stole fire from heaven for the benefit of mankind. The meaning is that the king, as Bolingbroke, assumed such an air of courtesy and regal behavior that he was thought to have won it directly from heaven, and thus to have robbed the gods of one of their special attributes.

Bavin: A bundle of useless brushwood. The king states metaphorically that the "shallow jesters" and "wits" who surround the "skipping" king indulged in constant meaningless jokes, which, like twigs, soon kindled and soon burnt out.

Carded: A metaphor borrowed from liquor-blending or inn-keeping. "To card" was to blend or mix two kinds of beer. In the present instance it has very much the same meaning as "Mingled his royalty with capering fools" in the following line.

Enfeoff'd himself to popularity: Gave himself up entirely to the pursuit of popularity. "To enfeoff" is a legal phrase meaning "to give possession of an estate;" one was said "to enfeoff" another with certain lands when he actually or constructively put the other in possession of them.

Lord Mortimer of Scotland: No trace can be found of any person under this name. There was a Lord March of Scotland (George Dunbar), who fought on the side of King Henry IV, and was the means of saving the king's life at the battle of Shrewsbury. Mortimer was the family name of the Earls of March of England, and is perhaps here applied inadvertently to the Scottish lord who bore a similar title.

ACT III • SCENE 3

Summary

At the tavern, Falstaff complains to Bardolph about how much weight he has been losing. He blames this entirely imagined loss on worry, and swears he will repent his sins. Bardolph agrees that he will worry himself to death. Thus, returns Falstaff, with characteristic logic, he must be made merry with "a bawdy song." He decides he has in fact been "virtuous enough" for a gentleman, having "sworn little," gambled only seven times a week, gone to a brothel only "once in a quarter-of an hour," occasionally paid back money he has borrowed, and generally lived virtuously. Bardolph insists that his behavior, like his size, has broken all bounds. Falstaff proposes that if Bardolph will "amend" his face (which is red and pock-marked, possibly from syphilis), he will amend his way of life, and he then bellows a series of insulting metaphors describing the size and redness of Bardolph's nose. The hostess, Mistress Quickly, enters and Falstaff aggressively asks her if she knows who picked his pocket the night before. Offended, she denies any knowledge of the affair and defends the honesty of her tavern employees. Rather heated give-and-take follows, with the hostess reminding Falstaff of the money he owes her. He again complains of being robbed in an establishment where he is so regular a customer, and claims that he has lost a valuable ring given him by his grandfather. The hostess says the prince has told her the ring is worthless, and Falstaff calls the prince a knave and a thief. With this, the prince and Poins enter, marching briskly as if to battle. The hostess tries to inform the prince of Falstaff's recent abuse of him, but Falstaff keeps interrupting her with questions about the war and about his pocket being picked. The prince dismisses the theft, and finally the hostess manages to report the insults and threats Falstaff has directed at him. Furious, Falstaff denies everything, describing the hostess in several thoroughly indecent ways. Hal laughingly defends Mistress Quickly and asks Falstaff to explain himself, which he evades doing with his usual tactics. Finally, the prince levels another set of insults at Falstaff for his heaviness and corrupt, lying nature. Falstaff wonders how, if Adam fell in an era of total innocence, he, Falstaff, should be expected not to fall in an era of total villainy. Hal now becomes more charitable, telling Falstaff that the money stolen at Gad's Hill has been repaid and that they must all go to the wars. He adds, to keep Falstaff from being too overjoyed at the news, that he has secured the old knight a commission in charge of foot soldiers so that he will have to walk to battle. Falstaff immediately begins to wonder where he can steal a horse. On an elated, military note, they all agree to meet the following day to receive their orders.

Commentary

This scene serves two somewhat contradictory functions in the play. A comic scene renewing the comic tone of Act II, Sc. 4, is clearly called for at this point. Following the scenes involving, first, Hotspur's chaotic world, then the king's, this scene swings the pendulum back to the world of comic detachment represented by Falstaff and the tavern. It deflates the tone of high seriousness and crisis that dominates the king-Hal exchange and, in part, the Hotspur-Glendower controversy.

But the scene is far from a carbon copy of the earlier comic episode, and the differences are significant in the overall movement of the play. For one thing, despite the continued brilliance of his wit, Falstaff is not drunk in this scene, neither literally nor figuratively. On the contrary, both Falstaff and the scene convey a distinctly "morning-after" effect, and as such, the scene suggests something of the effect of this play's sequel, *Henry IV*, Part II, in which Shakespeare seems to intend both the comic and historical portions to be suffering a hangover. In the earlier scene, the stress appeared to be on Falstaff's creative genius. The prince and Poins, as straight men, prepared the way for his greatest theatrical performance — re-enactment of the fictitious battle at Gad's Hill. Since the straight men were thoroughly dishonest in their roles, no moral reproach of any sort is associated with Falstaff's magnificent lies and evasions. The Falstaff we see in Act IV, Sc. 3, is more genuinely disgruntled than he was earlier. His attacks on Bardolph and the hostess are spoken in anger and irritation. And his spirit of conversion opening the scene, for all its obviously artificial qualities, suggests, at least, dissatisfaction with the *status quo*.

The pace of the scene picks up markedly with Hal's vigorous entrance. Whereas Falstaff's entrance clearly enlivened the earlier scene (Act II, Sc. 4), Hal's enlivens this one. Still dominated by an attitude of amused detachment, Hal now also reveals a sense of commitment his earlier appearances have lacked. As a result, though Hal is still the straight man, he is no longer subordinate to Falstaff in creating the dominant tone of the scene. He sounds the military note — they must all prepare to defend their country:

> The land is burning; Percy stands on high;
> And either we or they must lower lie.
>
> (Act III, Sc. 3, 194-195)

The scene concludes with a zest which is hardly of Falstaff's making, even though his final lines embody it:

> Rare words! brave world! Hostess, my breakfast, come.
> Oh, I could wish this tavern were my drum!
>
> (Act III, Sc. 3, 196-197)

Hal has brought this new spirit to the tavern, and has done so as a result of his sobering talk with his father. It is no longer the Falstaffian contempt for honor which keynotes the dialogue, nor the romantic honor of Hotspur, but the new clear-headed honor of Hal, which will ultimately lead to the greatness of his reign.

Notes

Apple-john: Sometimes referred to as "john-apple," it was a species of apple which ripened late but was famous as a "keeper," though when kept long its skin assumed a very shrivelled appearance.

A brewer's horse: The point in this simile is elusive, unless it is meant that a brewer's horse is apt to become lean and shrivelled (like the apple-john) from hard work.

Compass: Falstaff uses the word in the sense of "measure" or "moderation." Bardolph jokingly uses it in reference to Falstaff's size, in regard to his bulk and circular measurement.

Dives: A name by which the rich man in the parable in the Gospel of St. Luke, 16:19-31, is generally known.

Links: Torches. In the days before the streets became illuminated, it was necessary for people who walked them by night to be accompanied by link-men or torch-bearers to light their way.

Salamander: A lizard which was thought popularly to be able to live in fire. Falstaff suggests that if he had not kept Bardolph supplied with sack, the fire would have died from his face.

Dame Partlet the hen: The *partlet* was originally an article of apparel worn by ladies of Elizabethan times. It consisted of a ruff or collar worn around the neck, but its actual nature is in doubt. *Partlet,* from the ruff of feathers around its neck, would be an apt name for a hen and a form of it, Pertelote, was, in fact, the name of that well-known hen in Chaucer's "Nun's Priest's Tale."

Dowlas: A coarse linen much used by the poorer classes in Elizabethan times; thus it would be much despised by the knight, Sir John Falstaff.

Bolters: Sieves used for dividing the coarser from the finer particles of flour. Falstaff wishes to impress upon the hostess, how coarse and rough was the linen of the shirts which she bought for him.

Denier: A French coin of extremely small value, being equal to one-twelfth of a *sou.*

A drawn fox: This refers to a fox hunted out of cover, and so put to his wits to find the best line of escape. The fox, proverbially sly and cunning, would under these circumstances exercise his power of deceit to the very utmost.

Maid Marian: Maid Marian was first represented as the associate of Robin Hood, but later appeared in the May-day revels as a low, degraded character usually dressed in male clothing. The wife of the deputy of the ward (i.e., the common council-man) the elected representative of a ward of the corporation, would be, of course, the essence of circumstance and respectability.

My drum: My recruiting place. Falstaff, with his great and cumbersome figure, wishes that he could raise his company without leaving the comfort of the Boar's-Head, instead of having to tramp about searching for recruits. Recruiting was invariably accompanied by abundant use of the drum.

ACT IV • SCENE 1

Summary

At the rebel camp near Shrewsbury, Hotspur opens the scene by heaping praise on his former adversary, but now close ally, the Scottish Earl of Douglas. A messenger brings a letter from the Earl of Northumberland, Hotspur's father, informing them that he is seriously ill, that he will not be able to join the rebellion, and that he does not feel he can trust anyone else to lead his forces. Astounded, Hotspur feels that his father's sickness will "infect / The very lifeblood of our enterprise," that it will be "a perilous gash" to their hopes. He suddenly changes his tune, however, claiming this development is for the best, since it would be foolish to let all their fortunes ride on a single battle. Douglas suports this view, but the more calculating Worcester fears that Northumberland's failure to appear will be taken by some as a sign of weakness. Sir Richard Vernon enters to report that he has seen the king's forces approaching in great numbers. Hotspur asks whether he has seen Prince Hal,

> The nimble-footed madcap Prince of Wales,
> And his comrades, that daffed [waved] the world aside
> And bid it pass?
>
> (Act IV, Sc. 1, 95-97)

To his surprise, Hotspur is informed that the prince is approaching in full chivalric splendor. Angered by Vernon's very flattering description of Hal, Hotspur dares Hal to come on and swears that he will combat the young prince whose name he shares.

> Harry to Harry shall, hot horse to horse,
> Meet and ne'er part till one drop down a corse.
>
> (Act IV, Sc. 1, 122-123)

But Vernon adds the final blow of the scene with news that Glendower, too, will be unable to reach them in time, and that the king's forces number thirty thousand. Hotspur valiantly asserts that he is ready to meet the opposition whatever their number, and "die merrily," if need be.

Commentary

This scene might appropriately be titled "The Rebels' Dismay." All that happens in it — the two defections and Vernon's description of

Hal — foreshadows the doom of Hotspur's cause. Whether or not Northumberland is really sick is a matter of historical uncertainty. Shakespeare has "Rumour" refer to him as "crafty-sick" early in *Henry IV*, Part II, though his actual appearance in that play is as an ill man. In any case, his failure to appear here is the most serious blow the rebels suffer. Hotspur is joined in his rash confidence by the steadfast Douglas, but the realist Worcester knows that victory normally goes to the side with the greater numbers, despite all the determination in the world. Hotspur's chivalric illusions blind him to the realities of battle. This scene implies that, had all the rebel forces appeared, their numbers might well have exceeded the king's, and the result of the battle might have been different from what it was. But Act III, Sc. 1, has already indicated that the rebellious forces are not united (Hotspur versus Glendower) and further suggests that harmony is not in the nature of rebellion. The defections here bear out the point. Hotspur's and Douglas's mighty and heroic sense of honor can accomplish great things, of course. Were there no similar qualities on the other side, they still might win. But their chivalric bravery is countered by Vernon's description of Hal. The opposition will not be without effective leadership. Hal will possess all that Hotspur and Douglas possess and also have the superiority of numbers to assure victory. Hotspur fails to realize, like King Richard II before him, that one cannot depend on one's God-given attributes to hold or achieve power. One must have political, which usually means military, strength.

Notes

As not a soldier of this season's stamp: No soldier now living should be so universally held in esteem. The metaphor is drawn from a coin recently "stamped" (minted) and put into circulation, which passes everywhere as currency, and is on that account highly valued.

Justling: "To justle" is used by Shakespeare to mean "to fight," "to encounter," "to jostle." Thus a "justling time" would be a time of strife or the clashing of arms. *Cf. The Tempest,* Act III, Sc. 2: "I am in case to *justle* a constable."

Reversion: A legal term denoting the estate which returns or reverts to the lessor at the termination of a lease granted by him.

Hair: Course, direction. Hair as a general rule lies on the skin in a particular direction. Shakespeare uses "hair" figuratively to denote the ends or aims toward which their attempts are directed. Any attempts which were against their intentions would thus be contrary to, or against the "lie" of, the hair. *Cf. The Merry Wives of Windsor,* Act II, Sc. 2: "If you would fight, you go against the *hair* of your profession."

That with the wind/Bated like eagles having lately bathed: To "bate" is a term of falconry meaning "to beat or flap the wings". This habit is especially noticeable after a bird has bathed. Shakespeare's intention in the simile is to express the anxiety of the rebel army to be "on the move." Just as a charger would "paw the ground" in its eagerness to be moving, so would a bird eager to fly bate its wings with the wind.

Mercury: The messenger of love was usually depicted with wings on his feet.

Pegasus: The winged horse of mythology.

The fire-eyed maid of smoky war: The goddess of war, known among the Romans as Bellona.

ACT IV • SCENE 2

Summary

On a road near Coventry, Falstaff sends Bardolph ahead for more wine, assuring him that he will be repaid for the money he lays out. Alone, Falstaff describes his activities as an impressment officer, one who has official authority to draft soldiers at will. Falstaff explains how he has misused this authority by accepting bribes from a hundred and fifty prospective draftees. He has singled out only those most needed at home — heads of families, sons of well-to-do farmers, bachelors about to be married — so that he may be assured they will pay anything to avoid military service. Having received his bribes, he has substituted the worst elements of society — beggars, disinherited youths, unemployed servingmen. Someone has asked him, he says, whether he has made up his army with rotting corpses, his soldiers are so thin. Most, he admits, he got out of prison. They are all half-naked, he adds, but will find clothes enough to steal from laundry lines through the countryside leading to battle. Prince Hal and Westmoreland enter on their way to Shrewsbury. Hal asks Falstaff where he ever found "such pitiful rascals" for his army. Falstaff indicates that the men will make good cannon fodder.

Commentary

Falstaff as the recruitment officer, while in no way reducing the quality and effectiveness of his satirical humor, was bound to have aroused bitterness in the hearts of an Elizabethan audience accustomed to the arbitrary nature of military drafting in the 1590's. The recruitment officer was all-too-nightmarish a figure to the populace of sixteenth-century England, and the bribery Falstaff describes was a common practice. Drinking, whoring, and stealing royal funds could only make the old knight more appealing to an audience of young journeymen and apprentices, but abusing authority to recruit troops would have detracted from Falstaff's popularity. This struck too close to home, as would Falstaff's response to Hal that his soldiers will make good cannon fodder ("good enough to toss, food for powder, food for powder"). Falstaff's actions here tend to reduce him to size. Honor, convention, and tradition are absolute necessities to good government and an orderly existence, but they must be seen in proper perspective. Falstaff is bitterly satirizing abuses in the system of military recruitment in medieval England, and this helps put things in perspective. But in acting out the role he is satirizing, he becomes a somewhat less appealing figure than he was.

Notes

This bottle makes an angel. The purchase of this bottle makes an angel spent on wine. The angel was a gold coin worth about ten shillings.

The king's press: The authority granted Falstaff to recruit his company by drafting men into the service in the name of the king.

In the painted cloth: It was a common practice to make use of pictures painted in oils on cloth for the decoration of the interior of dwellings.

An old faced ancient: "Ancient" is used by Shakespeare to mean an ensign or officer who carries the standard, and also to mean the standard itself.

ACT IV • SCENE 3

Summary

In the rebel camp, Hotspur and Douglas argue with Worcester and Vernon over the best time to engage the enemy in battle. The former feel they should do so immediately, the latter that they should wait. They are interrupted by the entrance of Sir Walter Blunt, spokesman for the king, whom Hotspur receives graciously, wishing that Blunt had joined their cause. Blunt reports the king's desire to know their grievances so that they might possibly avoid the conflict. Hotspur answers that the king knows how to make promises and break them, as he has done to the Percies (Northumberland, Worcester, and Hotspur), who put him on the throne and received little thanks for it. In a long and heated speech Hotspur recalls the story of Bolingbroke's successful usurpation of the throne. He also refers specifically to the king's failure to ransom Mortimer and to Worcester's banishment. (See Act I, Sc. 1.) Blunt asks whether he should report all Hotspur has said to the king, but Hotspur, suddenly more cautious, says only that Worcester shall return Blunt's visit to report the rebels' grievances to the king.

Commentary

The situation opening the scene is later to be repeated in *Julius Caesar*. Hotspur, like Brutus, is rash in wishing to engage in immediate combat. The more cautious Worcester, like Cassius, wishes to wait for a more opportune moment. But it is, ironically, Worcester who ultimately proves rash, and Hotspur sensible, reversing the situation in *Julius Caesar* where Brutus started as the sensible one and Cassius was given to quick and rash decisions. Blunt's speech as messenger is measured and patient, clearly indicating that the king is ready to negotiate. Hotspur's response is bold and defiant, reminiscent of the fiery young knight in Act I, Sc. 3 and Act III, Sc. 1. But at the end he sends Worcester to talk. We can only assume that he has sensed honor in Blunt's remarks and is ready to listen. He is also, of course, aware deep down of the rebellion's weakness. The implications of this slight modification in Hotspur's tone are to be immediately significant.

Notes

To sue his livery: To claim, as heir of John of Gaunt, the delivery or possession of his lands from the Court of Wards, which, in feudal times, on the death of any tenant of the crown, seized and kept lands until the heir "sued out his livery."

To lie forfeited: Refers to a hostage or captive who was not ransomed by his friends and might linger indefinitely in captivity.

ACT IV • SCENE 4

Summary

The Archbishop of York (Richard Scroop), one of Hotspur's allies, and his friend Sir Michael discuss the rebellion's prospects. The Archbishop expresses concern that, without Northumberland and Glendower, their hopes for success seem slim. The Archbishop then sends messages to his own men by Sir Michael warning that should the king be victorious at Shrewsbury, which now seems likely, Henry will turn his attentions to them and they must be ready.

Commentary

Aside from its presentation of the historically renowned Richard Scroop, the rebellious Archbishop, this scene has little to do directly with the action of the play. It is the kind of episode that has been called a "mirror scene," a scene outside the main action or plot which focuses attention directly on a theme or idea underlying the action. The scene involving the violent death of Cinna the Poet in *Julius Caesar* is such a scene. It focusses attention on the blind irrationality of an inflamed mob. The present scene is a clear indicator of Hotspur's defeat. If so fanatic a rebel as Scroop feels the cause will be lost at Shrewsbury, the outcome is certain. The damage to the rebels' cause done by the absence of Northumberland and Glendower goes beyond the immediate prospects for the battle itself. It affects the unity of the broad, national movement which is ready to depose Henry. The scene suggests that events have broken the back of the whole rebellion, even before the battle has been fought.

ACT V • SCENE 1

Summary

In the king's camp, Worcester and Vernon, as messengers from the rebels, return Blunt's visit. The king asks them whether the rebels, instead of bringing war and bloodshed to the land, will change their course and again become loyal, trusted subjects. To Worcester's claim that he has not sought the present state of affairs, the king asks how, then, it has come about. Falstaff, an unexpected participant in the scene, bellows: "Rebellion lay in his way, and he found it." He is quickly hushed by Prince Hal, and Worcester commences his long speech listing the rebels' grievances. He restates much of what Hotspur said to Blunt, namely the king's supposed break of faith with the Percies following his decision to seek Richard's crown when no one thought he wanted more than his dukedom back. The king suggests that these claims have all been repeated many times, that what has been said is nothing but decoration to beautify "the garment of rebellion," which is wrong regardless of how one attempts to make it appealing to disgruntled and misguided subjects. The prince steps forward and proposes that he and Hotspur settle the matter through personal combat, but the king, assuring Hal of his confidence in him, feels that such a confrontation would be inappropriate. He sends Worcester back with the message that if the rebels will throw down their arms, all will be forgiven. Worcester having departed, Hal predicts that the offer of amnesty will be rejected.

Left alone by the king and his attendants, Falstaff instructs Hal that, if the prince sees him down in battle he should stand over his body to protect it (an ancient convention by which a warrior defends a friend fallen in battle). Hal insists it would take "a colossus" to do Falstaff that service, and departs, reminding Falstaff that he will one day die anyway, that he owes God a death. Falstaff's response is perhaps his best remembered in the play:

> 'Tis not due yet, I would be loath to pay him before his day. What need I be so forward with him that calls not on me? Well, 'tis no matter; honor pricks me on. Yea, but how if honor prick me off when I come on? How then? Can honor

set to a leg? No. Or an arm? No. Or take away the grief of a wound? No. Honor hath no skill in surgery then? No. What is honor? A word. What is that honor? Air — a trim reckoning! Who hath it? He that died a Wednesday. Doth he feel it? No. Doth he hear it? No. 'Tis insensible then? Yea, to the dead. But will it not live with the living? No. Why? Detraction will not suffer it. Therefore I'll none of it. Honor is a mere scutcheon — and so ends my catechism.

(Act V, Sc. 1, 127-139)

Commentary

Worcester's visit to the king parallels, in form and spirit, Blunt's visit to the rebels a scene earlier. It is formal and full of diplomatic protocol. Hence, it is the more surprising and unexpected for Falstaff, not only to break in as he does, but even to be present at the proceedings. He is a member of the nobility, of course, and an associate of the Prince of Wales. Nevertheless his comment breaks into the formal, serious dialogue in verse which has characterized all the "historical" scenes (as opposed to the comic scenes) throughout the play. His comment at this time and place signifies that the two opposing attitudes of the play — the comic and the chivalric — have finally met face to face. Falstaff's satire of convention and tradition is here applied directly to the historical action of the play. The irony of the remark is particularly suited to Worcester, whose approach to rebellion is hardly a matter of chance ("Rebellion lay in his way, and he found it!"), but is rather the result of cold calculation. Hal's offer to settle the conflict in personal combat with Hotspur is in keeping with the image of Hal which emerged in his dialogue with the king in the third act. Yet despite assurances of confidence, it seems clear that the king does not yet feel sure of Hal's success against Hotspur. The prince has yet to prove his new-found honor.

Nowhere in this play or its sequel does Falstaff express his anti-chivalric attitudes so clearly and brilliantly as here. To him, the honor which prompts the warriors around him to do battle and perhaps die is nothing, merely a word. A dead man who possessed it when alive is not better off than one who did not. It can accomplish nothing in this life, yet it can bring one an early death since it can tolerate no insult, real or imagined.

Falstaff's view, for all its wit and precision, represents an extreme. He dismisses all honor in his "catechism," not only the pure-to-a-fault honor of Hotspur, but the honor Hal is to represent throughout the remainder of this play and the two which follow it. In this act, it is Hal rather than Hotspur who counters the Falstaffian view, and in so doing, he demonstrates that view as ultimately no more acceptable than the Hotspurian one. Honor may, in fact, be more than "a mere scutcheon" if it is held by someone who fully understands its uses and limits.

Notes

Our old limbs: According to historical fact, Henry IV was not more than 37 years old at this time.

An exhaled meteor: A wandering meteor, supposedly from the exhalations of the sun and earth (in contrast with the placid planets moving in their apparent orbits) was an omen of disaster.

Peace, chewet, peace: In old cook books, "chewets" are fat, rich puddings or pies made of mince meat, cream, etc., and it is possible that the epithet is here applied to Falstaff as if to say, "You fat greasy pudding." Some commentators think that it is equivalent to the French *chouette,* a chough or daw, and is used in the sense of "chatterer."

The seat of Gaunt: Bolingbroke, son of John of Gaunt, on the death of his father became entitled to claim the dukedom of Lancaster, for which purpose he returned to England from the exile decreed upon him by Richard II. His succession to the dukedom is "His new-fallen right" of the previous line.

ACT V • SCENE 2

Summary

Back in the rebel camp, Worcester warns Vernon not to report the king's "kind offer" of amnesty to Hotspur, since the king, despite the offer, will never be entirely forgiving. Hotspur's crimes, because of his reputation for rashness, might ultimately be forgotten, he says, but Worcester and Vernon will be credited with having egged him on and will finally have to "pay for all." Hotspur and Douglas enter and are informed that the king has invited them to do battle immediately, that the king's response to Worcester's having told him "gently of our grievances" has been to call them rebels and traitors. Douglas responds defiantly, and Hotspur, hearing of the prince's offer of single combat, says he wishes the conflict could be settled in that fashion. He asks whether Hal was proud and contemptuous in his challenge, and Vernon again describes the prince in the most flattering terms:

> No, by my soul. I never in my life
> Did hear a challenge urged more modestly,
> Unless a brother should a brother dare
> To gentle exercise and proof of arms.
> He gave you all the duties of a man;

Trimmed up your praises with a princely tongue;
Spoke your deservings like a chronicle;
Making you ever better than his praise
By still dispraising praise valued with you.
And, which became him like a prince indeed,
He made a blushing cital of himself,
And chid his truant youth with such a grace
As if he mast'red there a double spirit
Of teaching and of learning instantly.
There did he pause; but let me tell the world,
If he outlive the envy of this day,
England did never owe so sweet a hope,
So much misconstrued in his wantonness.

(Act V, Sc. 2, 51-68)

Hotspur, as he did before, responds furiously to Vernon's description, accusing Vernon of being "enamored" of the prince's "follies," and referring again to Hal's reputation as a libertine. But, Hotspur warns, Hal will soon be shown who is the better soldier. A messenger brings letters, but Hotspur says he has no time to read them now. He appeals to his followers to fight to the death for their cause. After another messenger informs him that the king's army approaches, Hotspur draws his sword, embraces his friends, and goes bravely to battle.

Commentary

Worcester's comments to Vernon suggest the utmost in cold, calculating falseness and obviously are intended to relieve Hotspur of some of the blame for the rebellion. But Worcester is also probably correct in his analysis of the situation, and is following his instinct for self-preservation. Hotspur's honor, truth, and fierce reaction to personal insult make him, in the last analysis, a poor politician but an immensely attractive figure. As a supremely crafty politician, Worcester knows that he will never be trusted, and that revenge will ultimately be sought against him rather than Hotspur. He has from the start been "the brains" behind the venture. (See Act I, Sc. 3.)

Another thing to note in the scene is Vernon's second flattering description of Hal, and Hotspur's response to it. These descriptions of Hal by Vernon (the other in Act IV, Sc. 3) serve as Hotspur's approaching nemesis or retribution, and his responses to them reveal fear and insecurity. As a chivalric gentleman, Hotspur has always dismissed any mode of life not centered around one's honor. Even in his lighter moments, Hotspur's great ego is in evidence. To be faced now with so flattering a description of, and a challenge from, one who has laughed at honor, who has in the past placed so base a thing as physical pleasure over so noble a thing as chivalry is almost more than Hotspur can bear. All this suggests, more than ever, that the Hotspurian view is outdated and that the true hero is modest. He is one who has learned to temper his sense of personal honor with a sense of reality, and in the process, he has learned to place national concerns above personal ones, to consider the needs of all his countrymen. In fighting Hotspur (and later in fighting the French), Hal will be fighting for his country rather than his name, for the people of the tavern as well as those of the court.

ACT V • SCENE 3

Summary

In battle, Sir Walter Blunt, dressed as the king (to minimize the possibility of the king's being killed), meets the fierce Douglas. Thinking he has met the real king, Douglas challenges him to yield or fight. Blunt fights, of course, and is killed. As Douglas rejoices at the greatness of his conquest, Hotspur enters and quickly identifies the victim. Enraged, Douglas swears he will kill everyone dressed like the king until he meets the real king. They go out as Falstaff rushes in, obviously escaping from the conflict. Seeing the dead body of Sir Walter, he observes, "There's honor for you!" He has, he tells us, led his forlorn troops through the heat of battle in hopes that they may be killed and he be able to collect their pay. Hal enters, flushed from combat and begs Falstaff to lend him his sword, asserting that many dead noblemen "are yet unrevenged." Falstaff claims that he himself has exceeded "Turk Gregory" in "deeds of arms," and that he has killed Hotspur. Hal denies this and again asks for Falstaff's sword, which the latter refuses to turn over since Hotspur is still alive. But, says Falstaff, "take my pistol," and he hands him a pistol case. Hal opens it to find a bottle of sack. Hal abruptly asks: "What, is it a time to jest and dally now?" He angrily throws the bottle at Falstaff and goes out. Falstaff vows to kill Hotspur if he finds him, but then adds that if he is fool enough to cross Hotspur's path, he knows what his fate will be. He dislikes, he says, the "grinning honor" of the dead Sir Walter. Falstaff will settle for life, dishonorable or not:

> Give me life, which if I can save, so;
> if not, honor comes unlooked for,
> and there's an end.
>
> (Act V, Sc. 3, 56-58)

Commentary

Douglas' tearing around killing everyone dressed as the king has the effect of caricature, intended or not, and in fact, the scene rather grimly brings together the serious and the comic in a fashion similar to

Hamlet's comments on the dead Polonius. The effect seems bitterly satirical. Throughout the play, Sir Walter Blunt has been a noble figure, respected by both sides, and his death hardly seems an occasion for the grim humor initiated by both Douglas and Falstaff. His death is clearly futile rather than heroic. He is both a sacrificial lamb to the wild, irrepressible Douglas (who out-Hotspurs Hotspur) and a case-in-point supporting Falstaff's views on honor. As for Falstaff, his leading troops to certain death in order to collect their pay continues the unpleasant turn his character took in the recruitment scene. There is nothing in this picture of battle to support the Hotspurian idealization of war, but at the same time, neither is there anything to support the Falstaffian denigration of it. Hal's role in the scene makes this apparent. Hal is clearly heroic and honorable. While Falstaff continues his "catechism" on honor, Hal is off avenging fallen warriors. The contrast is important. Falstaff's satire hits home when applied to Hotspur and Douglas, but not when applied to Hal. Yet Hal appears in the scene, refusing for the first time to share in Falstaff's scornful fun. Something very important has changed in the Hal who asks, "What, is it a time to jest and dally now?" And with this change comes a revitalization of the concept of honor which could invite mockery when represented by Hotspur and Douglas with their entirely ego-centered approach to it, but not when represented by Hal with his balanced approach to it.

Notes

Shot-free at London: A play on the word shot, which here means without having to pay the reckoning which was "scored" against him at the tavern.

Turk Gregory: An allusion to Gregory VII, called Hildebrand, who before he was pope, was a most valiant and adventurous fighter.

Pierce: The pronunciation of the word "pierce" as used by Shakespeare rhymes with "rehearse" (*cf. Richard II,* Act V, Sc. 3, 127), and is here used as a pun on the word "Percy". (*cf.* also *Love's Labour's Lost* Act IV, Sc. 2, 86), where Shakespeare uses it as a pun on the word "person."

Carbonado: This word was used to describe a method of preparing a piece of meat for cooking. This preparation consisted of hacking and slicing the meat with a sharp knife. (*cf. King Lear*, Act II, Sc. 2: "Draw, you rogue, or I'll so *carbonado* your shanks.")

ACT V • SCENE 4

Summary

The king suggests that Prince Hal has too serious a wound for him to continue in battle, but Hal insists that "a shallow scratch" will not drive him from the field. Prince John claims they have rested too long and goes out with Westmoreland. Prince Hal speaks admiringly of his younger brother, admitting that he had never thought him "lord of such a spirit." The king says he saw John battle even Hotspur briefly. Hal goes out and the king is suddenly joined by Douglas, who wonders whether he has found the real one this time. The king assures him he has, and the two fight. As Douglas appears to be getting the upper hand, Hal returns and rescues his father. The proud and boastful Douglas runs away. The king assures him that in this rescue Hal has completely regained his lost reputation and disproved the rumors that he wished the king's death. Hal regrets the serious wrong done him by these rumors. The king goes out, and Hal is suddenly joined by Hotspur. They briefly exchange remarks, each claiming superiority in arms. Hotspur says he wishes Hal's "name in arms" were as great as his. They fight, and as they do are observed by Falstaff, who cheers Hal on. Falstaff in turn is attacked by Douglas and soon falls down pretending to be dead. Hal mortally wounds Hotspur, who, in a speech cut short by death, mourns the loss of reputation. Hal finishes the speech with words he knows Hotspur would have used, and does honor to the fallen hero, commenting on the inevitable irony involved in the death of so active and spirited a man. Then he sees Falstaff on the ground apparently dead and regrets that "all this flesh" could not "keep in a little life." He goes out leaving Falstaff to lie by the dead Hotspur.

With Hal's departure, Falstaff rises, swearing that "'twas time to counterfeit" death or Douglas would have "paid" him the real thing. But he wonders why he should call his action "counterfeit" when the true counterfeit of a man is a corpse, who looks in all ways like a man but is not. To pretend to be dead but really be alive is to be no counterfeit, he says, and adds the much-quoted (or misquoted):

> The better part of valor is discretion,
> in the which better part I have saved my life.
>
> (Act V, Sc. 4, 118-119)

Noticing Hotspur, Falstaff gets the idea that perhaps he "should counterfeit too." To reassure himself, he stabs the dead body anew and says he will claim Hotspur rose again and that he, Falstaff, killed him in personal combat. Prince Hal re-enters, along with Prince John, and to his surprise sees Falstaff carrying the body of Hotspur away. Seeing them, Falstaff throws the body down and says he expects honors from the king for having killed his enemy. Angrily, Hal says he himself killed Hotspur and saw Falstaff dead. Falstaff's response is characteristic and highly reminiscent of the tavern scene (Act II, Sc. 2):

> Didst thou? Lord, Lord, how this world is given to lying. I grant you I was down, and out of breath, and so was he; but we rose both at an instant, and fought a long hour by Shrewsbury clock. If I may be believed, so; if not, let them that should reward valor bear the sin upon their own heads. I'll take it upon my death, I gave him this wound in the thigh. If the man were alive, and would deny it, zounds! I would make him eat a piece of my sword.
>
> (Act V, Sc. 4, 142-149)

Hal answers that, if Falstaff wishes, he will gladly support his claim of having killed Hotspur, even though it is a lie. They hear a trumpet signalling the end of the battle and total victory, and Falstaff looks forward to the greatness about to be thrust upon him.

Commentary

Everything in this scene focuses on the emergence of Hal as the play's hero and dominant figure. In the early part of the scene Prince John's determination and courage, nobly complimented by his still unproved elder brother, recalls the king's insults to Hal in Act III, Sc. 2:

> Thy place in council thou hast rudely lost,
> Which by thy younger brother is supplied . . .
>
> (Act III, Sc. 2, 32-33)

Which son is the true "hope and expectation of the time" will shortly be revealed.

Hal's gradual elevation from ne'er-do-well to national hero is continued in the rescue of his father from the bloody hand of Douglas. The king is a brave and hardy warrior, but he is plagued by guilt and has also seen better days. He can no longer save his nation from harm by his own strength, both because of his sins and his declining years. With a display of skill and heroism, Hal, young and free from involvement in his father's crimes, overshadows the king as the dominant figure on the side of the state. Without Hal, the king, the head of state, would have been cut down, and with him, inevitably, all hope of unity and order. The figure of the king is an indispensable symbol in the maintenance of unity. Hal here single-handedly preserves that symbol and, at the same time, totally rehabilitates himself in his father's eyes, and thus in his country's eyes.

The real death of Hotspur paralleled with the "counterfeit" death of Falstaff also seems rather obviously to be symbolic action. The representatives of the two conflicting attitudes of the play engage in parallel struggles, the one to die courageously at the hands of a stronger adversary, the other to pretend death disgracefully at the hand of a boaster and bully. Hal, the emerging hero, leaves them lying together "in blood." The personal excesses of chivalric honor and its total denial are both swept aside before a new honor, tempered with Falstaffian wit and vitally concerned with national, not personal, pride.

Falstaff's "resurrection" is as necessary to the play as is Hotspur's death. True honor either triumphs or dies (as does Sir Walter Blunt). Dishonor can never triumph. Now that the image of the new honor (Hal) has been seen standing between the fallen figures representing the play's two extremes, it is time for the comic extreme to reassert itself. If death itself is the final pretence ("for he is but the counterfeit of a man who hath not the life of man"), then there is no need for Falstaff's death to be genuine. In his case, the semblance of death is enough. Falstaff's claim to having killed Hotspur, of course, allows Hal one of the two clearest and most emphatic displays of what is signified by the new honor. Despite all that the defeat of Hotspur means to Hal and to the country, Hal will gladly "gild" Falstaff's story "with the happiest terms" he has. The quickest way to realize the significance of Hal's response here is to consider what Hotspur's would be under similar circumstances. Certainly Hal is generous and good-natured in agreeing to honor Falstaff's claim to glory. Hal willingly goes along with the jest for two possible reasons. For one thing, Falstaff makes the claim, and nothing he says need be taken seriously. But more important, once the pressure is off and the nation is no longer in danger, Hal can in part assume his former nature. In short, what Hal possesses that Hotspur lacked is perspective, and perspective is what is crucially needed for successful leadership.

Notes

Hydra's heads: In Greek mythology, Hydra was a monstrous dragon with nine heads. When one was cut off, two grew in its place. One of Hercules' twelve labors was the slaying of Hydra.

The wound my thoughts . . . Dr. Samuel Johnson thus explains this passage: "Hotspur in his last moment endeavours to console himself. The glory of the prince *wound his thoughts* but *thought,* being dependent on life, must cease with it, and will soon be at an end. Life, on which *thought* depends is itself of no great value, being the tool and sport of *time,* of *time* which with all its dominion over sublunary things must itself at last be *stopped.*"

Ill-weaved ambition: Shrunken ambition; a metaphor taken from the manufacture of cloth, which shrinks when woven too loosely.

Let my favors hide . . . The word "favors" signifies gifts as tokens of respect or love, and in the present instance probably consisted of a scarf worn by the prince.

Termagant: Termagant was a Saracen deity introduced as a violent and passionate character into the Miracle Plays. (*cf. Hamlet,* Act III, Sc. 2, 15.)

Had paid me scot and lot too: To pay "scot and lot" is a legal expression signifying payment of rates or other parochial contributions. It is here used for the sake of the play on the word "scot," and means simply that Douglas would have "paid" Falstaff enough blows to have ended him.

ACT V • SCENE 5

Summary

The victors enter, led by the king, with Worcester and Vernon as prisoners. For their disloyalty, coupled with their (really Worcester's) treachery in misrepresenting the king's message to Hotspur, the king instructs that they be put to death. Prince Hal asks that he may dispose of Douglas, to which the king readily agrees. Hal then instructs Prince John to see that Douglas, for his honor in battle, be freed without ransom. The king then divides his forces in order to meet his still-unconquered foes, Northumberland, Scroop (the Archbishop of York), and Glendower. The king's closing lines refer to the theme that unifies all Elizabethan history plays:

> Rebellion in this land shall lose his sway,
> Meeting the check of such another day;
> And since this business so fair is done,
> Let us not leave till all our own be won.
>
> (Act V, Sc. 5, 41-44)

Commentary

Worcester and Vernon are put to death in traditional fashion, Worcester perhaps deserving this fate, but not Vernon, who has been so eloquent in his praise of Hal and otherwise "borne himself nobly." It may be that, as Worcester's second, his fate is appropriate. But how does it compare to Douglas' fate at the hands of Hal? Hal's action represents a bold departure from tradition. Prisoners could expect two alternatives in medieval warfare, execution or imprisonment for ransom. Douglas escapes both. The battle done, he is treated like an ally who has fought bravely. Battles, for Hal, concern political not personal issues, and once the political end is achieved, the individual opponent may keep his honor intact. In his later actions as king leading his forces in France (*Henry V*), Hal will respond similarly. That this play is a transitional one, however, and that much remains to be done to assure unity in the kingdom is signified by King Henry's final lines preparing his followers for the battles to come.

Characters

Methods of Analyzing Characters

Dramatic character is a product of many diverse elements. Most of these elements should be considered in any careful estimate or description of any character. They are listed below.

Position or Role

Is the character rich or poor, nobleman, tradesman or servant? Is he an old man or youngster, illegitimate offspring or head of a family, vying sibling or sole heir? Shakespeare showed great discernment and subtlety in his awareness of the typical attributes of the various ages and sexes, and many of them are notable in this play.

Comments About a Character

Much of Shakespeare's characterization depends on what others say about a character or what the character says about himself. Hotspur, for instance, is not introspective. He says nothing about his own personality, but the comments of Worcester, the king and Prince Hal add a definite contribution to our understanding of him.

Character Motivation

The style and content of any statement give us a clue to the personality and motivation of the character who speaks, whether he intends it or not. The ornate rhetoric of the king, the monstrous exaggerations of Falstaff, and the beauty of Hotspur's tribute to destruction all help to characterize them.

Even more indicative are a character's actions. Frequently his actions conflict with and disprove his words. Falstaff's claims to bravery go up in smoke before his cowardly behavior, and the king's claims of benevolent concern are undercut by his faithless treachery.

The words and deeds of a character lead us to estimate his ruling motives. These may be displayed outright at the beginning of the play, or they may be revealed gradually, remaining unclear until a crucial exposure. For instance, Worcester's essential motives are not clear until his betrayal of Hotspur, but the revelation is damning.

Thematic Characters

Some characters take on a thematic value in Shakespeare's plays. For instance, Iago in *Othello* represents a spirit of pure evil which seems to transcend any specific motivation that might lead him to behave as he does. This is an example of a crude, rather simplistic thematic character. Hotspur and Falstaff are also thematic, but they are far more subtle and complex, and the forces or attitudes they represent are difficult to define.

Relations to Other Characters

A character analysis, to be complete, must consider the relations of the character to all the others of the play. Falstaff's significance in *Henry IV* cannot be evaluated without considering his relations to Prince Hal. If he were not one of the rebels, Hotspur would take on an entirely new position and meaning.

Character Sketches

King Henry the Fourth

In this play, a close insight into the personal character of the king is not given, though certain features of his character are pronounced. The features which are depicted by the dramatist are certainly not attractive, and one has an impression throughout the play that every word and action of the king is based on insincerity and scheming deliberation, rather than on honesty and impulse. Shakespeare draws an effective contrast between the king and Harry Hotspur; the former cool, calculating, and insincere, the latter hot-headed, impulsive, blunt and honest. Between these two extremes he places Henry, Prince of Wales, his hero, who possesses the virtues of each, but does not share their vices. Prejudice against the king is constantly aroused. One is reminded of the cruel and unscrupulous means he employed to gain possession of the throne, of the arrogant manner in which he overrides opposition, of his erroneous judgment of his son's character, and the consequent antagonism against his son caused by this error of judgment. Whatever may be thought of King Henry's character and motives, it must be admitted that his is a powerful personality; he is a man full of determination and perseverance; he possesses the power to make an instant decision and to act on that decision without delay; he is a firm supporter of his own maxim:

> Advantage feeds him fat while men delay.
>
> (Act III, Sc. 2, 180)

A MAN OF ACTION

When the play begins, the king is contemplating an expedition to the Holy Land with the avowed object of supplying his subjects with a topic of interest which would act as a counter-attraction to the recent trouble which culminated in his usurpation of the throne. The news of the battle of Holmedon and of the rising of Owen Glendower entirely frustrates his plans for a crusade, and he is compelled to turn his attention to the more pressing emergencies within his own kingdom. He is at once spurred to action. His plans to defeat the rebels are made without confiding in or consulting any advisers, and he takes immediate action in accordance with his plans (Act III, Sc. 1, 170). Taking the field with his army, he begins the campaign with the greatest vigor (Act II, Sc. 1, 90). The actual attack of the rebel forces is commenced immediately on the return of Worcester and Vernon, the envoys of the Percies, to their leader (Act V, Sc. 1, 118). On his discovery that Worcester and Vernon had misused their office as messengers, he gives them scant consideration, and after the battle sends them to their death (Act V, Sc. 5, 14).

HIS DIGNITY

The king never for one moment relaxes his kingly bearing. He always bears in mind that he is a ruler of men and that he must be "ne'er seen but wonder'd at." He himself gives us a clear perception of what he considers should be the correct attitude of a monarch to his subjects:

> Had I so lavish of my presence been,
> So common-hackneyed in the eyes of men,
> So stale and cheap to vulgar company,
> Opinion, that did help me to the crown,
> Had still kept loyal to possession
> And left me in reputeless banishment,
> A fellow of no mark nor likelihood.
> By being seldom seen, I could not stir
> But, like a comet, I was wond'red at;
> That men would tell their children, 'This is he! '
> Others would say, 'Where, which is Bolingbroke? '
> (Act III, Sc. 2, 39-49)

A SCHEMER

Though Harry Hotspur is a prejudiced speaker, one must almost agree with him when he refers to King Henry IV as a "Vile politician" (Act I, Sc. 3, 241), a "king of smiles" (Act I, Sc. 3, 246), a "fawning greyhound" (Act I, Sc. 3, 252), and a proud king who would study day and night in order to devise plans for the overthrow of anyone hostile to him. The king himself admits that his "condition" is dictated purely by policy, and that he merely "dress'd" himself in a guise of humility in order to "pluck allegiance from men's hearts" (Act III, Sc. 2, 51).

THE KING AND HIS SON, THE PRINCE OF WALES

In the opening scene of the play the king expresses his keen disapproval of the character and mode of life of his son, the Prince of Wales, comparing him to his great disadvantage with Harry Hotspur.

Yea, there thou mak'st me sad, and mak'st me sin
In envy that my Lord Northumberland
Should be the father to so blest a son —
A son who is the theme of honor's tongue,
Who is sweet fortune's minion and her pride;
Whilst I, by looking on the praise of him,
See riot and dishonor stain the brow
Of my young Harry.

(Act I, Sc. 1, 78-86)

It is clear that the waywardness of "young Harry" causes his father great pain; yet one also has the impression that the pain is caused not so much by reason of his natural affection for his son, but rather by reason of the loss of dignity which he himself suffered on account of his elder son's wildness. Harry Hotspur recognises this strained attitude between father and son, and that "his father loves him not / And would be glad he met with some mischance" (Act I, Sc. 3, 231). Later in the play, Shakespeare makes it clear that this strained attitude was due purely to the unprincely behavior and apparent disloyalty of the prince, and not to any lack of natural affection on the part of the king. When the king is in trouble and threatened with civil war, the prince immediately breaks with his companions of the tavern and flies to his father's assistance, proving to the world by his deeds that his loose life was rather due to his exuberance of spirit than to any evil in his character. The prince on the battlefield is a character which the king can understand. He recognizes the reformation and vividly displays by his anxiety his concern for his son:

. . . Harry, withdraw thyself; thou bleedest too much.
Lord John of Lancaster, go you with him.

(Act V, Sc. 4, 2)

Later in the same scene he admits that the prince, whom he is now proud to call his son, has reinstated himself in the king's regard by his loyalty:

Stay and breathe awhile.
Thou hast redeemed thy lost opinion,

(Act V, Sc. 4, 47)

Henry, Prince of Wales

Son to the King

The most interesting and rounded character in the play is undoubtedly Henry, Prince of Wales. No other character drawn by Shakespeare is so many-sided. He is versatile even to the extent of inconsistency, and it is this inconsistency which makes his character so natural and full. In him one observes a young man, almost a youth, high-spirited, perfectly natural, whose will is sufficiently strong to enable him to cast convention aside, to resist the traditions which govern the behavior of the heir apparent, and to defy all the efforts of his father and the court to make him live his life according to the dignity befitting one who might become a king. The flattery and insincerity of court life give him no opportunities for fulfilling his craving for a natural life with its excitement. In order to give vent to his high spirits, he becomes a member of a certain dissolute section of society where he can be a man among men, and be quite free of conventions.

THE PRINCE OF WALES AMONG HIS COMPANIONS

The first impression of the prince one receives in the play is the comparison drawn by his father between him and Harry Hotspur, and the heart-felt sigh of the king that "riot and dishonor stain the brow of my young Harry." This introduction naturally prejudices the reader against the prince, and prepares him for an idle, time-wasting, knavish, tavern-frequenter. The first appearance of the prince confirms our initial judgment of his character. He is seen joking with the roguish knight, Sir John Falstaff, who later in the same scene incites him to "take a purse." The first token in the play that the prince is not so debased as his father believes is the expression of intense indignation which escapes him when Falstaff invites him personally to take part in the thieving expedition:

Fal: Hal, wilt thou make one?
Prince: Who, I rob? I, a thief? Not I, by my faith.
(Act I, Sc. 2, 128-129)

In spite of his horror at being associated with such a dishonorable act as stealing, he does not criticize Falstaff for organizing such a raid. He takes his companions as he finds them and makes no endeavor to change their mode of life. Before the prince has time to withdraw from the plot, Poins interposes and suggests to the prince a plan whereby not only will Falstaff be embarrassed, but also the spoils of the intended robbery will be returned to their rightful owners. Poins' plot appeals to the prince, as it promises even more excitement and humor than the original expedition and, moreover, it is undoubtedly more honorable. The appreciation of a good practical joke is one of the features of the prince's character. He is quite unable to resist the fun promised by Poins' suggestion, which succeeds entirely according to design and culminates in the rollicking scene at the Boar's-Head Tavern, Eastcheap, in which he teases Falstaff, and the latter is forced to his wit's end to excuse himself. The prince, having turned the thieving expedition into a source of amusement for himself, feels that he should take all the responsibility for the breach of the law, and when the sheriff appears with his men to apprehend Falstaff and his gang, the prince acts as their protector, and postpones the sheriff's operations against them for a time sufficiently long to enable the goods to be returned to those from whom they were stolen.

Laughter, good humor and practical jokes are the essence of the prince's companionship with Falstaff. The prince is generally ready to crack a joke or have fun with him, but whereas Falstaff is never able to control his sense of humor which intrudes at most unexpected times, the prince has a keen appreciation of the fitness of things and never allows his role as a joker to interfere with the more earnest side of his life. Note how the prince reproves Falstaff sternly for attempting a joke during the struggle with the rebel forces:

> What, is it a time to jest and dally now?
>
> (Act V, Sc. 3, 54)

The reader of the play has an advantage over the king in judging the prince's character. From what one gathers from the play, the king was never intimate with his son and never saw or heard his son when surrounded by his wastrel companions. His imagination would lead him to believe that the prince was living a worse life than was actually the fact. The father never experienced one of those earnest moments of the prince, when after a more vivid bout of revelry than usual, he remained alone on the scene of the revelry and let his thoughts bear on the more serious side of his life. These are the moments when Prince Harry discloses his real self; then one sees that, though he has been among his companions joining in the merriment, he was never one of them. He always remembers that he is passing idle hours with them until more serious events should claim his attention:

> I know you all, and will awhile uphold
> The unyoked humor of your idleness.
> Yet herein will I imitate the sun,
> Who doth permit the base contagious clouds
> To smother up his beauty from the world,
> That, when he please again to be himself,
> Being wanted, he may be more wondered at.
>
> (Act I, Sc. 2, 183-189.)

THE PRINCE OF WALES AS HERO OF THE PLAY

Shakespeare makes the prince the central character of the play and the whole plot is based on his misunderstanding with his father due to his dissolute life and the subsequent reconciliation brought about by his noble bearing when fighting against the rebels for the royal cause. Shakespeare's Prince of Wales is an heroic character, revealing every virtue and devoid of all vice. Courage, modesty, good humor and generosity are his most striking features.

HIS COURAGE

The courage of the prince is displayed in the play for the first time while he is still an associate of his idle companions of the tavern. Though he must have been fully aware that Falstaff, Gadshill, Bardolph and Peto are at heart cowards, it requires considerable courage to attack them, with only Poins to assist him, and rob them of the goods, which they had stolen from the travellers. Though wounded in the earlier stages of the battle against the rebel army, and commanded by the king to withdraw himself from the fight because of his wounds the prince subsequently engages in personal combat with the famous fighters, Douglas and Harry Hotspur. The former is put to flight by the fury of his onslaught and the latter is killed by the prince.

HIS MODESTY AND CHIVALRY

His bravery is emphasized by his modesty and his chivalrous treatment of his opponents. Vernon's descriptions of the prince's challenge to Hotspur give a clear conception of the dignity and bearing of the Prince of Wales as a future ruler of the realm, as contrasted with Hal, the associate of Falstaff:

I never in my life
Did hear a challenge urged more modestly,
Unless a brother should a brother dare
To gentle exercise and proof of arms.
He gave you all the duties of a man;
Trimmed up your praises with a princely tongue;
Spoke your deservings like a chronicle;
Making you even better than his praise
By still dispraising praise valued with you;
And, which became him like a prince indeed,
He made a blushing cital of himself;
And chid his truant youth with such a grace
As if he mast'red there a double spirit
Of teaching and of learning instantly.

(Act V, Sc. 2, 51-64)

His quiet dignity and his forgiving nature are well illustrated by his attitude at the side of the body of Harry Hotspur:

this earth that bears thee dead
Bears not alive so stout a gentleman.

(Act V, Sc. 4, 91-92)

HIS GENEROSITY

The prince's attitude towards his tavern companions undergoes a complete change when he severs his companionship with them to undertake the serious task of helping to subdue the rebellion. In spite of this change, he never forgets his friendship with them, but puts them in positions of trust in the royal army.

Falstaff in particular is favored by the prince, who not only gives him authority to raise a company, but also allows him to steal the credit for the death of Harry Hotspur.

The prince again displays his generous nature by not only forgiving and obtaining a pardon for Douglas, but surrendering to his younger brother Prince John the honor of announcing the pardon to Douglas.

HIS VERSATILITY

One of the most remarkable features of Prince Harry is his versatility. He is seen playing practical jokes on the tapster of a tavern (Act II, Sc. 4); he is seen indulging in revels with his immoral companions; and yet again in solemn conference with the great nobles of the land, including his father, the king. In any company he always appears perfectly natural; there is no affectation in his character. Though the prince appears in his element when plotting vulgar jokes to play on fat Falstaff, he is admirably described by Vernon who is reporting to Harry Hotspur:

> I saw young Harry with his beaver on,
> His cushes on his thighs, gallantly armed
> Rise from the ground like feathered Mercury,
> And vaulted with such ease into his seat
> As if an angel dropped down from the clouds
> To turn and wind a fiery Pegasus
> And witch the world with noble horsemanship.
>
> (Act IV, Sc. 1, 104-110)

Prince Harry and Harry Hotspur

Shakespeare draws an effective contrast between the characters of these two men. The chief characteristic they have in common is their valor, though the valor of Harry Hotspur is of the hot-headed, arrogant and boastful type, whereas that of the prince takes the form of a cool, calm confidence in his own powers. Compare Hotspur's violent and arrogant attitude with regard to the battle (Act IV, Sc. 1) with the modest and calm demeanor of Prince Harry (Act III, Sc. 1). One can have only admiration for the characters of both men, though the prince's manner in expressing his emotions is entirely contrary to the manner adopted by Harry Hotspur. The former is appealing in his calm, deliberate and modest nature, whereas the other is attractive and repellent at the same time because of his combination of high spirit and arrogance.

Prince John of Lancaster

Son to the King

During the period when the Prince of Wales was in disfavor with his father, his younger brother, Prince John, took his place in the state councils. He plays an unimportant part in the play, and is chiefly notable for his chivalrous and gallant bearing in the fight with the rebels (Act V, Sc. 5). He is chosen by the Prince of Wales to inform the defeated and captured Douglas that he has been pardoned and is "ransomless and free." (Act V, Sc. 5)

Earl of Westmoreland

Friend to the King

He announces to the king in the first scene of the play the "heavy news" from Wales concerning the rebellion led by Glendower against Mortimer and his Herefordshire men. King Henry places him in charge of a contingent of the royal forces. (Act III, Sc. 2).

Sir Walter Blunt

Friend to the King

Sir Walter Blunt is a knight in the retinue of King Henry and is in constant attendance on his majesty. He is sent to the Percies by the king as envoy before the battle, and is particularly fitted for the task as he is held in great esteem by both forces. Harry Hotspur, who certainly cannot be said to be generous with praise, assures him when on that errand that:

Some of us love you well; and even those some
Envy your great deservings and good name.
(Act IV, Sc. 3, 34-35)

He takes an exceedingly active part in the battle and is one of the valorous knights who impersonate the King during the battle in order to prevent any attack in force on the king's person. While performing this dangerous and gallant office he meets his death at the hands of Douglas.

Thomas Percy

Earl of Worcester

The king banishes Worcester from his court and councils. The King sees "danger and disobedience" in his eye, and regards him from his "bold and peremptory" presence as one not to be trusted (Act I, Sc. 3). Subsequent to this dismissal Worcester becomes one of the chief conspirators against the king. Hotspur himself admits that Worcester is a powerful ally and that his plans are "well aim'd" (Act I, Sc. 3). He is present during the dispute among Hotspur, Mortimer and Glendower concerning the partition of territory, and preaches a small sermon to Harry Hotspur, pointing out the necessity of curbing his rash temper (Act II, Sc. 1). Immediately before the battle, he is rather pessimistic about the prospects of the rebels, owing to the absence of the Earl of Northumberland, Hotspur's father, and in spite of Hotspur's protestations that his father's absence would not be vitally prejudicial to the rebel cause, Worcester still maintains that:

> This absence of your father's draws a curtain
> That shows the ignorant a kind of fear
> Before not dreamt of.
>
> (Act IV, Sc. 1, 73-75)

Worcester maintains his opinion in a vigorous protest, in which he is joined by Vernon. They want to wait until all the rebel forces have been gathered and are ready for battle, but this protest is over-ruled by the hot-heads, Hotspur and Douglas (Act IV, Sc. 3). In the first scene of the last act, Worcester with his companion, Vernon, appears before the king as envoys from the rebel forces, and Worcester seizes on this opportunity to urge his personal grievances against the king. In the following scene Worcester and Vernon reveal their villainy by misinterpreting wilfully the message of the king to the leaders of the rebel forces. This false report of the attitude of the king leads directly to the battle, which might have been avoided had "the liberal and kind offer of the king" been faithfully conveyed. Both the delinquents reappear in the last scene, when they pay the penalty for their treachery.

Henry Percy

Earl of Northumberland

This is the father of Harry Hotspur, and one of the rebel leaders. He is prevented by illness from assisting in the battle. Even after the decisive defeat of the rebels at Shrewsbury, he still maintains a state of active rebellion, and in the closing words of the play, the king directs:

> You, son John, and my cousin Westmoreland,
> Towards York shall bend you with your dearest speed
> To meet Northumberland and the prelate Scroop,
> Who, as we hear, are busily in arms.
>
> (Act V, Sc. 5, 35-38)

Henry Percy

Surnamed Hotspur, Son of Northumberland

The essence of Hotspur's character is impulse, making him a most vivid foil to the more deliberate Prince of Wales, who, though quick to think and act, never indulges in that rash, unthinking and violent wilfulness of his rival. Hotspur is violent when, in similar circumstances, the prince would be calm and reasonable. He is a devoted searcher for that "mere scutcheon," honor, and all his actions are directed with impulsive energy in its pursuit. Hotspur is so governed by his craving for honor, and his impulse in pursuit of it, that he enters into any mad act without thought of the consequences. The sense of proportion and the sense of humor which are so prominent in the character of the prince are entirely lacking in Hotspur.

HIS COURAGE

His foremost characteristic is his courage. He is the hero of the battle at Holmedon, where he completely devastates the Scottish champion, the Earl of Douglas, thereby exciting the envy of King Henry:

> Yea, there thou mak'st me sad, and mak'st me sin
> In envy that my Lord Northumberland
> Should be the father of so blest a son —
> A son who is the theme of honor's tongue,
> Amongst a grove the very straightest plant; . . .
>
> (Act I, Sc. 1, 78-82)

In the pursuit of his obsession, honor, his courage knows no bounds and his keenest wish is:

> Send danger from the east unto the west,
> So honor cross it from the north to south,
> And let them grapple. O, the blood more stirs
> To rouse a lion than to start a hare!
>
> (Act I, Sc. 3, 195-198)

He yearns for a bloody fight:

> O, let the hours be short
> Till fields and blows and groans applaud our sport!
>
> (Act I, Sc. 3, 298-299)

Falstaff seems mistaken in ranking Hotspur with that "fiend" Douglas and that "devil" Glendower (Act II, Sc. 4). When the three rebels are considered together, Hotspur towers above them. His personality is so powerful that they seem but puppets to do his bidding. He anticipates his fight to the death with the prince with eagerness, and only regrets that the prince's name in arms is not as great as his own so that he might add the prince's honors to his own if he proved to be victorious.

HIS PRIDE AND AMBITION

The argument with Mortimer and Glendower in the first scene of the third act concerning the division of territory by the tripartite agreement gives a clear insight into Hotspur's general temperament and, particularly, into the persistence of his pride. Rather than concede the minutest point, he would beggar himself:

> I'll give thrice so much land
> To any well-deserving friend;
> But in the way of bargain, mark ye me,
> I'll cavil on the ninth part of a hair.
>
> (Act III, Sc. 1, 135-138)

His pride in his own honor and achievements at times becomes indistinguishable from haughty arrogance. Even when mortally wounded, his mental anguish at his own defeat is greater than the physical torture of his wounds:

> I better brook the loss of brittle life
> Than those proud titles thou hast won of me.
> They wound my thoughts worse than thy sword my flesh.
>
> (Act V, Sc. 4, 177-179)

HIS GENEROSITY

His loyalty to his friend Mortimer can only be attributed to impulsive generosity. Not only is he willing to part with his possessions "to any well-deserving friend" who may have fallen on evil days, but he is willing to sacrifice even life itself in the cause of his friend Mortimer, who, he believes, has been harshly treated:

> Speak of Mortimer?
> Zounds, I will speak of him, and let my soul
> Want mercy if I do not join with him!
> Yea, on his part I'll empty all these veins,
> And shed my dear blood drop by drop in the dust, . . .
>
> (Act I, Sc. 3, 130-134)

HIS ENERGY AND STRENGTH OF PURPOSE

His energy is amazing, and though the prince exaggerated grossly when joking against Hotspur (Act II, Sc. 4), there is much truth in his anecdote.

It is clear that Shakespeare intended to convey to hearers of this play that the conspiracy to rebel against King Henry IV would never have been contemplated, nor would it have succeeded even as well as it did, if not for the strong character and powerful driving force of Hotspur.

HOTSPUR AS A HUSBAND

Regarding (from a purely sentimental point of view) Hotspur's attitude towards his wife as depicted in this play, one is struck immediately by his apparent callousness. He is essentially a man of action, very impulsive, who scorns any suspicion of sentiment or even courtesy for the sake of courtesy. Throughout this play we see him with serious business in mind; this serious business he will not allow to be interrupted in any way by less serious matters. His mind is set, with one fixed purpose before it, though he swears that so long as no deviation from this fixed purpose is caused by his affection for his wife, he will love her "infinitely." When parting from her, he makes the promise that "whither I go, thither shall you go too," (Act II, Sc. 3) and trusts that this promise will content her. Though we never have a glimpse of Hotspur with his wife in the absence of turmoil and trouble, we can imagine him, under ordinary circumstances, as an impulsively chivalrous and affectionate husband.

Edmund Mortimer

Earl of March

He appears in only one scene of the play, the first scene of the third act, in which he acts as peacemaker in the dispute between the fiery Hotspur and the braggart Glendower.

Richard Scroop

Archbishop of York

He appears in person in only one scene (Act IV, Sc. 4). Reference is made (Act I, Sc. 3, 277) to the plot to cause him to throw in his lot with the rebels. The Earl of Worcester urges that he would be a ready recruit to the cause of the rebels against King Henry, because he "bears hard/His brother's death at Bristol, the Lord Scroop."

Archibald

Earl of Douglas

His main characteristics, bravery, chivalry and in a minor degree, arrogant bluster, are very similar to those of Hotspur, though he by no means possesses Hotspur's commanding personality, and is quite content to play second fiddle to him. He is taken prisoner in the battle, but set at liberty again through the generosity of Prince Hal.

Owen Glendower

Unreasoning vanity is the chief feature of this Welshman, who claims that at his birth "The frame and huge foundation of the earth / Shaked like a coward." He possesses none of the bluff and hearty dignity of Hotspur or Douglas. He brags about what he will do, but his actions fail to confirm his words. His boastful vanity has little weight in the dispute with Hotspur and Mortimer over the division of territory. He is completely dominated by their more powerful personalities.

Sir Richard Vernon

One of the messengers of King Henry, who wilfully misinterprets the king's message to the leaders of the rebels. He pays the penalty for his treacherous action by being sentenced to death.

Sir John Falstaff

Probably the most popular character in British drama, the "fat knight" is familiar and acclaimed throughout the civilized world. The great Italian composer, Verdi, made the adventures of Falstaff the theme of what is generally considered his greatest opera. Even in his own time Shakespeare found that Falstaff was such a popular character on the stage that he introduced him into several of his plays, and in order to ensure the success of one of his plays (*Henry V*), he promised the audience in the epilogue of a previous play (*Henry IV,* Part II) that he would introduce Sir John as one of the characters.

Libertine, braggart, thief, coward, glutton, liar, drunkard, he is physically and morally repulsive. He is so fat and short of breath that on the least exertion he "sweats to death and lards the lean earth as he walks along" (Act. II, Sc. 2). Where, then, is the secret of his popularity? Falstaff is undoubtedly a rogue, but a rogue who appeals not only to our sense of the ridiculous, but also to our sense of humor. We laugh at his nimble wit, and his rogueries are confused with his jests. He is perfectly honest concerning his wickedness and only jokingly attempts to assume a virtue which he does not possess. His wit, his astounding presence of mind, his unfailing good humor, his tremendous capacity as a clown are the secrets of his personality. His subtle wit, his blatant buffooneries, so unexpected in a man with his gross, unwieldy body, are the secrets of his popularity.

William Hazlitt, the eminent eighteenth century writer and critic, had this to say about Falstaff:

> The unrestrained indulgence of his own ease, appetites, and convenience has neither malice nor hypocrisy in it. In a word, he is an actor in himself almost as much as upon the stage, and we no more object to the character of Falstaff in a moral point of view then we would think of bringing an excellent comedian, who should represent him to the life, before one of the police offices. We only consider the number of pleasant lights in which he puts certain foibles (the more pleasant as they are opposed to the received rules and necessary restraints of society), and do not trouble ourselves about the consequences resulting from them, for no mischievous consequences do result. Sir John is old as

well as fat, which gives a melancholy retrospective tinge to the character; and by the disparity between his inclinations and his capacity for enjoyment, makes it still more ludicrous and fantastical.

Poins, Gadshill, Peto and Bardolph

The Dissolute Companions of Falstaff

Poins seems much more intelligent and less immoral than the others comprising this tavern-frequenting crew. It is Poins who invents the practical joke on Falstaff and suggests it to the prince who carries it out, to the utter humiliation of Falstaff and his friends. Poins, in the execution of this joke, steals Falstaff's horse and, with the prince, deprives Falstaff of the plunder of which he robbed the merchants and which is subsequently restored by the prince to its rightful owners. Poins always treats the prince with respect, which is not shown to him by Falstaff and the rest of his companions.

Gadshill plays the part of "setter" or spy to Falstaff's band of robbers, and discovers from the chamberlain of the inn and the carriers the movements of the franklin who is carrying "three hundred marks with him in gold." Gadshill verifies Falstaff's imaginative account of the robbery and the fight which follows.

In this play, Bardolph has a small part and merely acts as a target for Falstaff's shafts of wit. In *Henry V,* he takes a much more important part and, as the dominating influence of Falstaff is absent, we can get a much truer idea of the baseness of Bardolph's character — a cowardly braggart, who ends his days on the gallows with Pistol, his sworn brother in theft. He is chiefly notable for the red, blotchy and unattractive coloring of his face.

Lady Percy

Wife to Hotspur and Sister to Mortimer

Hotspur's Kate appears in only two scenes of the play but leaves a memorable impression. Beyond her first speech, which must be reckoned as a false start, she is a spirited and affectionate wife to Hotspur. However, she contributes nothing to the action, serving primarily as a foil for Hotspur. Notice that in their scenes together this husband and wife take on precisely the same emotional mood, using the same tone of sarcasm and bantering affection. Shakespeare uses these scenes and Lady Hotspur herself as musical interludes to interrupt the action and refresh the audience.

Lady Mortimer

Daughter to Glendower and Wife to Mortimer

Lady Mortimer, like Lady Percy, does not play an important part in the action. The value of the presence of Lady Percy among the characters in the play is that she gives us an insight into the more intimate side of the character of her husband, Hotspur. Lady Mortimer appears only in Act III, Scene 1. She takes no part in the dialogue, as she neither speaks nor understands the English language. However, she sings a song in her own language, Welsh.

Mistress Quickly

Hostess of a Tavern in Eastcheap

Falstaff and his knavish associates spend their idle hours drinking and carousing in the Boar's-Head Tavern, Eastcheap, of which Mistress Quickly is hostess. She takes no part in the action of the play except to act as a butt for the coarse jests and heartless rogueries of Falstaff. Having a weak nature she falls very easily into Falstaff's traps. At one moment he throws her into a violent rage with his jokes at her expense, but can with flattery immediately smooth her ruffled feathers. Her brain does not work rapidly enough for her to realize that Falstaff only speaks or acts to serve his own selfish ends. Falstaff even persuades her with flattery to lend him money and to purchase clothing for him (Act III, Sc. 3).

Questions and Answers on Characters

Question 1.

Who is the king of the thieves at the Boar's-Head Tavern?

Answer

At first glance, Falstaff would seem to be the king of the thieves. He sets the tone of their society, he talks the loudest and most often, and he is the oldest. Yet a careful investigation reveals that the prince has the upper hand over Falstaff and controls the group. At Gad's Hill, the prince, in alliance with Poins, defeats the rest of the thieves and steals their booty, and it is obvious that Poins follows the leadership of Hal, for he conceives and executes the plot with him and later in the tavern the two of them carry out a scheme against the tapster at Hal's instigation.

In the robbery, Bardolph and Peto act with Falstaff, but at the prince's request they expose the old man's tricks without a moment's hesitation. Clearly, the members of the band are more loyal to Hal than to Falstaff. The older Knight is bested by the young prince again and again. He is outfought in the duel at Gad's Hill (Act II, Sc. 2), and his lies about it are exposed by Hal (Act II, Sc. 4). Hal must save the sleeping Falstaff from the sheriff (Act II, Sc. 4) and having done so he robs him again (Act II, Sc. 4).

Later, in an argument with Falstaff about the second theft, Mistress Quickly uses Hal as an authority in refuting Falstaff's lies about the stolen ring. And Hal again, as "the robber who knows," exposes the exaggerations of his friend, who must apologize to Mistress Quickly.

The prince establishes his superiority over Falstaff by robbing him twice, exposing his lies and protecting him from the consequence of his follies. The members of the gang affirm this superiority by their loyalty to the prince.. In these respects the prince, not Falstaff, must be considered the king of the thieves.

Question 2.

The characterization of Hotspur's wife, Lady Percy, in Act II, Sc. 3, undergoes an abrupt change. Describe her "two personalities," identify where the change occurs, and give an explanation for it.

Answer

When Lady Percy first appears in Act II, Sc. 3, she addresses Hotspur as "O my good lord" and speaks in very elegant, poetic language. Instead of asking him simply why he ignores her, she asks "what is't that takes from thee/ Thy stomach, pleasure and thy golden sleep?" and "Why dost thou bend thine eyes upon the earth . . . ?" She elaborates simple ideas into complex metaphors; she uses poetic instead of colloquial words. Using her opening speech for a basis of characterization, we would assume her to be dignified, and full of poetic airs and graces, a perfect heroine. Later, however, the style of her address changes completely. Having been ignored by her husband, she now resorts to common epithets and a simple direct colloquial style.

> Out, you mad-headed ape!
> A weasel hath not such a deal of spleen
> As you are tossed with. In faith,
> I'll know your business, Harry, that I will!
>
> (Act II, Sc. 3, 74-77)

Her conversation with her husband remains the same for the rest of the scene and in the other scene in which she appears. Since Lady Percy's character must be based on her speeches with Hotspur (her part in the action of the play is insignificant), it may be assumed that she undergoes a change, which begins in Act II, Sc. 3, 81. Her conduct after this point establishes her as an affectionate, informal and spirited girl. She is fond of her husband, but her curiosity and gentle nagging show that she is not the least subdued with him, will fight for what she wants, and obviously does not stand on dignity.

In the light of her later more important characterization it is hard to explain her beginning speech. Considering the woman and her relation with her husband, she could give such a speech only with tongue in cheek; yet its language gives no indication of irony or satire. One may only guess at the reason for the discrepancy. Shakespeare probably started the scene without a clear notion of her character. He reached for a lyric grace to contrast with Hotspur's abruptness, but later dropped it when his imagination took over and the picture of the two squabbling lovebirds began to take shape.

Question 3.

Define the precise nature of Worcester's relation to Hotspur as revealed in the play.

Answer

In the first scene of the play, Westmoreland suggests that Worcester, out of his hatred for the king, has goaded Hotspur into refusing the king his prisoners. This is the first indication that the older man uses his nephew for his own purposes. Later, in the third scene, while pretending the contrary, Worcester fans the anger of Hotspur against the king, claiming that Henry hates Mortimer because the latter was declared legal heir to Richard's throne and emphasizing the scandal of the Percy family in aiding Henry to the throne. After Hotspur's anger has subsided, Worcester presents a detailed plan of rebellion and strengthens Hotspur's determination by saying that the king will dispose of the Percies if they do not dispose of him first. It is obvious now that Worcester manipulates the impetuous Hotspur as a pawn.

Later in Act III, Sc. 1, Worcester backs Hotspur when he fights for a larger portion of the land the rebels are planning to divide. Later he scolds the younger man for his wilfulness in arguing with Glendower over the same subject:

> In faith, my lord, you are too willful-blame,
> And since your coming hither have done enough
> To put him quite beside his patience.
> You must needs learn, lord, to amend this fault.
> Though sometimes it show greatness, courage,
> blood —
> And that's the dearest grace it renders you —
> Yet oftentimes it doth present harsh rage,
> Defect of manners, want of government,
> Pride, haughtiness, opinion, and disdain; . . .
>
> (Act III, Sc. I, 175-183)

It is fatherly advice, and one might assume up to this point that Worcester manipulates his nephew to aid the young man and further the Percy family. But it seems curious that the older man would urge the younger on and then blame him for the very excesses he has encouraged. But Worcester's true colors are revealed when he returns from the parley with the king and hides the king's last-minute request for peace. His reasons are clear:

My nephew's trespass may be well forgot;
It hath the excuse of youth and heat of blood,
And an adopted name of privilege —
A hare-brained Hotspur, governed by a spleen.
All his offenses live upon my head
And on his father's. We did train him on;
And, his corruption being ta'en from us,
We, as the spring of all, shall pay for all.
(Act V, Sc. 2, 16-23)

Finally his motives are evident. Worcester manipulates Hotspur not for Hotspur's good, and not for the good of the Percy family, which will sink to utter and complete defeat if the battle is lost, but merely to save himself. He openly admits this in the last scene of the play, offering no excuses except his own safety. Notice Worcester's response to the king's condemnation:

King: Three knights upon our party slain to-day,
A noble earl, and many a creature else
Had been alive this hour
If like a Christian thou hadst truly borne
Betwixt our armies true intelligence.
Worcester: What I have done my safety urged me to.
(Act V, Sc. 5, 6-11)

Style

Methods of Analyzing Style

In the work of every good writer there are stylistic qualities which can be easily defined, but there are always others which defy analysis. The critic can do no more than set up certain analytic guidelines, and hope that these will illuminate the most important qualities of a writer's style. Therefore, various general aspects of style are mentioned below. They may serve as a point of departure, and perhaps encourage the student to discover other elements on his own.

Diction

Words are the basic building blocks of the language, and a writer's style is largely determined by the words he uses. Certain questions may clarify his word preferences and the ways in which they influence his style. Are they long Latin words like "experience" and "acquaintance" or short Saxon words like "hurry" and "friend?" Are they abstract like "honor," or concrete and sensuous like "apple?" Are they typical of the vocabulary of aristocrats, tradesmen or servants? Are the words appropriate to a bar-room, a family meal or a coronation? Are they rich in poetic and emotional connotations, like "maid" and "lass" and "broad," or are they merely useful words like "girl?"

Grammar

Contrary to traditional education of the past, there is no one "correct" method of conveying meaning in the English language. There are a variety of methods, all quite successful, even though some are not accepted in the best circles and on the most dignified occasions. For instance, when the carrier responds to Gadshill's request to borrow his lantern, he speaks most incorrectly in terms of proper grammar:

> Aye, when? Canst tell? Lend me thy lantern,
> quoth he? Marry, I'll see thee hanged first.

Even today, we must struggle to get his meaning, because "Aye when? Canst tell?" in Elizabethan England was an expression of disbelief, something like our "Says you!" But to a carrier of that time, the meaning would have been perfectly evident. The point is that grammar, the verbal structure by which we convey meaning, changes from class to class, and from one time to another.

Shakespeare was a master of proper grammar and the various grammatical styles of the different classes as well, but he also distorted and stretched grammatical connections in his *own* ways. He used nouns for verbs and verbs for adjectives; he joined words in unusual ways; he omitted words we would consider essential today. Some of these things he did to preserve the meter of his lines, others to concentrate and enrich his meaning. But these grammatical devices figure largely in the "style" or "styles" of Shakespeare.

Rhetoric

Beyond the connections of grammar are the figures of speech which, although rare today, held an important place in Elizabethan literature. Generally speaking, the figures gave added grace and significance to the language by special arrangements of words or sounds. Among them were certain verbal structures you may have already studied, such as "hyperbole," "synecdoche," "antithesis," etc. But other, more complicated figures of speech were common in Shakespeare's day, and he used them to good advantage. Frequently they set the tone or style of a passage.

Imagery

Two figures of rhetoric, the metaphor and simile, present analogies. Both compare one thing to another, and so allow the writer great freedom in choosing material for his comparison. A woman accompanied by her admirers may be compared by an author to a gentle wind full of birds, to the progress of a great ship with its tenders, to a garbage wagon surrounded by flies. The possibilities are endless, and the ways in which a writer uses this freedom of imagery help establish his style.

Aesthetic Qualities

Besides its capacity to communicate meaning both at the abstract and concrete levels, language also conveys a range of emotional and aesthetic feelings which are not strictly central to the message. There is a world of difference between "A bird sang at sunset" and "The bird-song rippled joyously over the hushed surface of the dying day." The two sentences *mean* essentially the same; only their feeling differs. This feeling may be characterized in different passages as lyric, solemn, pathetic, comic, sinister, ironic — in brief, by as many moods and emotions as the mind of man can register.

In characterizing the style of a passage, however, it is necessary to be more specific than this. For instance, if a passage is melancholy, how does it achieve that affect? In the choice of words, in the rhythm of language, in the imagery, or in the subjects referred to?

Rhythm

Rhythm, particularly in poetry, is an integral element in the effect of any style. In poetry we must consider meter, while in prose we must consider the length of the sentences, clauses and phrases. Notice in this play that Shakespeare casts certain speeches in poetry and others in prose. For instance, Hal speaks prose with Falstaff and poetry with the king. Here, Shakespeare uses a difference in rhythm to mark a distinction in the dignity and elevation of the communication.

Styles of *Henry IV*, Part I

It has been said that Shakespeare contained multitudes; he therefore contained a multitude of styles. It is almost impossible to isolate and define the Shakespearean style. *Henry IV,* Part I is representative of his works, for it includes an enormous range of classes, personalities and, consequently, an amazing variety of styles.

The Falstaffian Style

The most notable style of the play is that of Falstaff. His cronies, Peto, Poins, Bardolph and Gadshill, all speak a similar, though less complicated, version of the style, and when the prince is with the gang, he outdoes even Falstaff. In spite of the impression it creates, this style is neither crude nor simple. On the contrary, it is supple, complex and amazingly ornate:

> What a devil hast thou to do with the time of day? Unless hours were cups of sack, and minutes capons, and clocks the tongues of bawds, and dials the signs of leaping houses, and the blessed sun himself a fair hot wench in flame-colored taffeta, I see no reason why thou shouldst be so superfluous to demand the time of the day.
>
> (Act 1, Sc. 2, 5-11)

The subjects may be "vulgar," but the images are carefully chosen. They are, at times, breathtaking in the surprise of their effect, and they are beautifully fitted in an elaborate figure, relating images of time to images of degeneracy.

If this style has a flaw, it lies not in art but in an excess of art, in exaggerations which stretch beyond the harmonious proportions of dignity and grace. This is a characteristic of Falstaffian temper and Falstaffian language as well. Excess is its keynote. Ornate images, based on the most unlikely analogies, are piled one on top of the other in chaotic abundance. Oaths are preferred to simple statements; numbers are exaggerated beyond all reason; and mere comparatives are always sacrificed to more exciting superlatives. Listen to the excesses of Falstaff's complaint about walking at Gad's Hill.

> . . . Well, I doubt not but to die a fair death for all this, if I scape hanging for killing that rogue [Poins]. I have forsworn his company hourly any time this two-and-twenty years, and yet I am betwitched with the rogue's company. If the rascal

have not given me medicines to make me love him, I'll be hanged . . . I'll starve ere I'll rob a foot further. An 'twere not as good a deed as drink to turn true man and to leave these rogues, I am the veriest varlet that ever chewed with a tooth . . .

(Act II, Sc. 2, 13-23)

By the same token, arguments mount to dizzy heights of frenzy and are rendered eloquent by savage epithets. These are never simple curses, but must be lovingly fashioned into the most unusual, grotesque and vilest shapes imaginable.

Prince: I'll be no longer guilty of this sin; this sanguine coward, this bed-presser, this horseback-breaker, this huge hill of flesh —
Falstaff: S'blood, you starveling, you eel-skin, you dried neat's-tongue, you bull's pizzle, you stockfish . . .

(Act II, Sc. 4, 229-233)

There are many puns that go into the making of the Falstaffian style, and these are frequently so subtle one must reread a passage to catch all of them. In the lines below, Falstaff is naming the leaders of the rebellion for Hal:

Falstaff: Owen, Owen — the same; and his son-in-law Mortimer, and old Northumberland, and that sprightly Scot of Scots, Douglas, that runs a horseback up a hill perpendicular—
Prince: He that rides at high speed and with his pistol kills a sparrow flying.
Falstaff: You have hit it.
Prince: So did he never the sparrow.
Falstaff: Well, that rascal hath good metal in him. He will not run.
Prince: Why, what a rascal art thou then, to praise him so for running!

(Act II, Sc. 4, 324-335)

The praise referred to occurred about ten lines back at the beginning of the passage, and forms the basis for this second pun on "running." The other pun on "hit" is more obvious. The interest of the pun, of course, lies in the unexpected use of one word in two different ways, and the sudden reversal of meaning shocks the listener into amusement.

This reversal of the expected stands beside exaggeration as the other important element in Falstaffian style; the puns depend on it. The epithets gain their humorous quality from the sheer unexpected novelty of the comparisons, and the parodies in which Falstaff and Hal indulge take advantage of both exaggeration and reversal, exaggerating the style to be parodied and rendering it more ridiculous by unexpected and incongruous elements which betray its surface tone. These include Hal's parody of Hotspur (Act II, Sc. 4), and the rehearsal between Falstaff and Hal (also in Act II, Sc. 4). In the latter, Falstaff, taking the part of the king, indulges in a style of royal oratory used frequently in the theater. In the process, Shakespeare not only exaggerates the solemnity and grandeur of the style, but punctures it periodically by an inappropriate word, a misplaced comment or an incongruous image. Such is the case when Falstaff, as king, must restrain the hostess, who has fallen into a giggling fit over the grandeur of his portrayal of royalty:

> **Falstaff:** And here is my speech. Stand aside, nobility.
> **Hostess:** Oh Jesu, this is excellent sport, i' faith!
> **Falstaff:** Weep not, sweet queen, for trickling tears are vain.
> **Hostess:** Oh, the Father, how he holds his countenance!
> **Falstaff:** For God's sake, lords, convey my tristful queen!
> For tears do stop the floodgates of her eyes.
> **Hostess:** Oh Jesu, he doth it as like one of these harlotry players as I ever see!
> **Falstaff:** Peace, good pintpot. Peace, good ticklebrain.
> (Act II, Sc. 4, 371-380)

In its exaggerated poetry and glaring incongruities, the passage aptly represents the Falstaffian style, which may cover any subject and embrace any tone as long as it is outrageously overdrawn, absurdly inconsistent, and betrays the sense of propriety at every turn.

The Noble Style

The language of the aristocratic elders has a special style of its own. It is spoken consistently by Vernon, Blunt, Westmoreland, the archdeacon and the elder Percies. Glendower speaks a slightly madcap version of it. The king speaks a more studied and ornate version. Even Hotspur and Prince Hal, when in court or in the presence of their elders, speak a less formal variant of the same. This is just one of the many styles Shakespeare fashioned from blank verse, but it has marked characteristics of its own. The sentences are long rather than short. The ideas tend to be abstract rather than matter-of-fact. Elaborate similes and metaphors are common, as are other ornate rhetorical figures of speech. The style is, however, seldom impassioned; it seldom breaks with the intensity of great emotion, or flutters with lyric grace. It sweeps and rises on the more measured winds of tempered emotion and reasoned eloquence.

How now, my Lord of Worcester! 'Tis not well
That you and I should meet upon such terms
As now we meet. You have deceived our trust
And made us doff our easy robes of peace
To crush our old limbs in ungentle steel.
This is not well, my lord; this is not well.
What say you to it? Will you again unknit
This churlish knot of all-abhorréd war,
And move in that obedient orb again
Where you did give a fair and natural light,
And be no more an exhaled meteor,
A prodigy of fear, and a portent
Of broachéd mischief to the unborn times?
(Act V, Sc. 1, 9-21)

This passage is typical of the king. The language of the other nobles differs only slightly. Glendower is, if possible, even more ornate and imaginative in his style, competing with Falstaff in excess. The other nobles speak a simpler, more direct style. However, a certain stateliness of tone is still unmistakable.

Worcester: It pleased your majesty to turn your looks
Of favor from myself and all our house;
And yet I must remember you, my lord,
We were the first and dearest of your friends.
(Act V, Sc. 1, 30-34)

Notice that the diction is less poetic, the imagery simpler, the sentences less complex; yet the rhythm of the verse and the cadences of phrases strike a tone of dignity and stately grace.

Functions of Style

Students often think of style as a spontaneous product of the writer's personality and training. More often it is deliberately achieved, and a writer like Shakespeare, who learned to master many styles, used style as deliberately as a painter uses color, and for as many purposes. The style of any passage cannot be fully understood without an awareness of the purposes for which it is used.

Style as Ornament

Shakespeare tried to render every passage of his plays not only useful and necessary, but ornamental and interesting as well. He rarely permits any lines to pass, no matter how necessary, without some aesthetic interest. Even the most humdrum exposition or dullest revelation of motive is granted some grace of wit, poetic feeling, rhetorical elegance or spicy slang. In the opening scene Shakespeare ornamented those expository lines with splendid and unforgettable images:

> So shaken we are, so wan with care,
> Find we a time for frighted peace to pant
> And breathe short-winded accents of new broils
> To be commenced in stronds afar remote.
> No more the thirsty entrance of this soil
> Shall daub her lips with her own children's blood:
> No more shall trenching war channel her fields,
> Nor bruise her flow'rets with the armèd hoofs
> Of hostile paces.
>
> (Act I, Sc. 1, lines 1-9)

With the exception of that somewhat disappointing fourth scene in Act IV, the whole play is of the same quality. Everything beautiful may not be necessary, but everything necessary is consistently rendered beautiful.

Style as Character

Style also has a function in characterizing each of the major personalities of the play. The gross exaggeration, the exuberant gusto and playfulness, the "vulgar" diction of Falstaff's speech certainly help us to understand the man. Notice that his speech is primarily expressive and suggestive. It seldom settles down to that primary work of language, which is to communicate facts. This highlights the immaturity of his character, which shuns the hard facts of objective reality for immersion in the subjective play of fantasy and self-absorption.

The abrupt simplicity of Hotspur's diction and the shortened elliptical phrases of his grammar help to paint his image as well. His character is further delineated when his attempt at the more courtly language of his elders comes out as an impetuous jumble of poetic images lacking in proportion and order.

Prince Hal's initial lack of style is also characteristic. That he reflects Falstaff's style simply means that his character is under Falstaff's influence for the time being. But at the end of the second scene in Act I, when left alone, Hal reverts to the blank verse of royalty. This significant shift indicates that, though under Falstaff's influence, Hal is not his man, but at the core a nobleman and prince. Finally, Hal's development in the final scenes of an easy yet dignified blank verse style as flexible as Hotspur's, yet more ordered and coherent, as logical and ordered as the king's, yet more spontaneous and natural, indicates the mature integration of his personality.

Style as Situation

Character and ornament, however, are not the only functional determinants of style. For just as individuals vary their personal styles to fit a given situation, so the characters in a play take on the prevailing tone or mood of a scene.

The Falstaffian style prevails in many scenes of the play, but not only because it is characteristic of one old man. It is a typical expression of the rough companionship of males, and Shakespeare has used the same style in other plays where Falstaff never appears. In this sense it is a situational style, appropriate wherever men relax and are free of civilized restraints. This is amply proven when Falstaff himself in the later scenes of battle, where crisis and hardship rule, departs from that style. Notice how simple and direct are his soliloquies at the end of the scenes in Act V. The monstrous exaggerations, the elephantine conceits, the grotesque images are all gone. What remains is a pithy, concrete exposition of the dilemma of honor and self-preservation.

It appears helpful, then, to dispense at times with the issue of style as character and view it as a function of situation. Certain styles are appropriate to certain situations and social groups: blank verse to court, Falstaffian prose to inns, a primitive style to innyards and ostlers, another more lyric style to lovers, and a hearty banter to the happily wed.

Style as Structure

In the first scene of the fourth act there is one of the most spectacular and poetic passages of the play, spoken by Vernon and Hotspur, although the language is not characteristic of either of them. While the poetry is one of the brightest ornaments of the play, sheer delight is not its only purpose. For its deeper function we must look to the structure of the scene, which is based on a testing and proof of Hotspur's resolution. In the process, four major objections against engaging in battle are presented to the young warrior, and before each he arises triumphantly unshaken.

These challenges to his determination occur in repetitive, wavelike rhythms of gradually increasing intensity. The first and second crises build until they reach the spectacular climax of the third, when a great wave of splendid poetry breaks over the ears of the audience and is answered by an equally splendid response from Hotspur. This is followed by a smaller repetition of the rhythm of challenge and response, closing the scene.

This satisfying structure would fall flat without the supercharged poetry which illuminates its climax, and the scene serves as a perfect example of the use of style to implement dramatic structure.

Questions and Answers on Style

Question 4.

Shakespeare employs a stylistic trick to close many of the scenes of the play. Tell what it is, why Shakespeare uses it and, if possible, when.

Answer

Shakespeare closes Act I, Sc. 1 and 2, Act III, Sc. 2 and 3, Act IV, Sc. 1 and 2, and Act V, Sc. 5, with rhymed couplets. Since there are only a few cases of rhyme in the whole play, this is an obvious literary device, deliberately intended. Just as a period signals the end of a sentence, these rhymes give a pat little thump which announces that the end of the scene has come. Therefore, the purpose of the device is structural rather than ornamental, situational or characterizing.

When the style in the final passage is prose, Shakespeare never resorts to the device, using it only as a complement to blank verse. In this respect, however, he is not entirely consistent. There are quite a few scenes ending in blank verse which do *not* end in a rhymed couplet, namely Act I, Sc. 1, Act II, Sc. 2 and 3, Act III, Sc. 1, Act IV, Sc. 3 and 4, and Act V, Sc. 2.

Question 5.

Analyze the following passage for style and describe the ornamental effect it creates.

> **Glendower:** She bids you on the wanton rushes lay you down
> And rest your gentle head upon her lap,
> And she will sing the song that pleaseth you
> And on your eyelids crown the god of sleep,
> Charming your blood with pleasing heaviness,
> Making such difference 'twixt wake and sleep
> As is the difference betwixt day and night
> The hour before the heavenly-harnessed team
> Begins his golden progress in the east.
> **Mortimer:** With all my heart I'll sit and hear her sing.
> By that time will our book, I think, be drawn.
> **Glendower:** Do so, and those musicians that shall play to you
> Hang in the air a thousand leagues from hence,
> And straight they shall be here. Sit, and attend.
> **Hotspur:** Come, Kate, thou art perfect in lying down.
> Come, quick, quick, that I may lay my head in thy lap.
> **Lady Percy:** Go, ye giddy goose.
>
> (Act III, Sc. 1, 211-227)

Answer

This passage has two basic styles: the first including Glendower's two speeches; the second, comprising the conversation of the Percies.

Glendower's passage is frankly poetic in a conventional sense. There are certain words which strike one as poetic diction: "wanton," "heavenly-harnessed" and "golden." But far more indicative of the poetic mood are the images. Instead of merely singing Mortimer to sleep, his wife will on his eyelids "crown the god of sleep." Dawn is described as "The hour before the heavenly-harnessed team/Begins his golden progress in the east."

The subjects of the passage are of the same mood and tone. The bride singing to her husband, whose head is in her lap, the mention of the dawn, the thoughts of sleep — all establish a gentle, romantic mood. Glendower's reference to the fairy musicians "a thousand leagues from hence" who will play for them, adds a touch of Welsh whimsy.

The second passage, spoken by the Percies, replaces this style for another. There is not a trace of poetic diction here, and although there is a wealth of imagery, none of it could be considered lyric in a conventional poetic sense. Hotspur's first sentence shocks us out of the romantic mood of the Welsh lovers. The sexual innuendo is unmistakable, and he proceeds in the second sentence to a double meaning less obvious but more outrageously obscene. Lady Hotspur gives an appropriately delighted and chiding response. It is pure slang: "Go, ye giddy goose." But even this is based on an image.

Curiously, then, the conversation of the Percies is more packed with imagery — and a variety of meanings — than the ostensibly "poetic" language of Glendower. It is important not to dismiss it as poetry, however, merely because the images, the diction and the subject matter do not fulfil our conventional sense of the "poetic." The style here is earthy, colloquial, sardonic and a little bit sly; but this is poetry all the same.

In summation, then, the total passage includes two smaller passages of contradictory style and content. The first deals with love in lyric and romantic terms. The second deals with the same subject, love, in an earthy humorous way. The close juxtapositon of the two styles creates an exquisite dramatic contrast.

Question 6.

Analyze briefly the following passage for style, and consider carefully the function of that style with respect to character, situation, structure and ornamentation and with particular regard to the rest of the scene (Act V, Sc. 1) in which it appears.

Falstaff: Hal, if thou see me down in the battle and bestride me, so! 'Tis a point of friendship.
Prince: Nothing but a colossus can do thee that friendship. Say thy prayers, and farewell.
Falstaff: I would 'twere bedtime, Hal, and all well.
Prince: Why thou owest God a death.

(Act V, Sc. 1, 121-126)

Answer

The diction of the passage is colloquial and straightforward. The grammar is simple and uncomplicated. The only distinguishing marks of the passage are the two examples of humor. Falstaff asks the prince to stand over and protect him if he falls in battle, and the prince replies that only a giant could do that, making an obvious dig at the clown's monstrous size. Finally there is wry humor in the prince's dismissal of Falstaff's fears, adding that the old man owes God a death.

In itself, the passage is a rather unremarkable example of the usual banter between the prince and his disreputable companion. As a matter of fact, there is a careful muting of the gaudy exuberance of the usual Falstaffian style. There are no puns, no lengthy metaphors, no complicated figures of speech here. The language is even a little straightforward, if compared to the wild freedom of the scenes in the Boar's-Head Tavern.

Nevertheless, the style contrasts markedly with the situation in which it occurs. This is the first scene of the last act, in which the battle is to take place. Shakespeare has already prepared, even in the opening lines, an atmosphere of foreboding and anxious unrest. The main body of the scene is taken up with the last minute negotiations between the king and Worcester. Negotiations have failed, and battle, with its threat of disaster and death, is imminent.

In direct contrast to this mood, the Falstaffian passage relieves the dramatic tension in three specific ways. First, it breaks the stately, tense style of the noble antagonists with a casual, more relaxed language. Second, it lightens the seriousness of the situation with a little humor. Third, it balances the almost inhuman stoicism of the warriors with a little genuine, spontaneous emotion. Falstaff's pathetic admission of fear, "I would 'twere bedtime, Hal, and all well," reminds us of the mortality of man. It offers a return to that more human honesty which the warriors do not show. For all these reasons the passage is aesthetically refreshing, just as a bright accent of contrasting colors adds life to an otherwise bare room.

The passage adds its little insight in terms of characterization. Falstaff is afraid — we expect that — and so are all the others, though they will not say it. But of all of them, he is the only one honest enough to admit it. There is no boasting now before the real crisis, and his simple expression of feeling lends him a pathetic dignity, sensed before only in his appeal for Hal's love.

The prince's response is stoic, apparently lighthearted and unconcerned. He expresses the dehumanized response of the other warriors. But he must, because to perform well in the battle he must completely repress fear.

The passage is most significant, however, in terms of structure. Its primary purpose is to prepare the audience for Falstaff's soliloquy at the end of the scene. In this sense, it is transitional, although, as noted, Shakespeare has rendered the transition both characterizing and ornamental. The structural problem is simply this: Shakespeare must get the audience from the formal, tense battle negotiations of the aristocrats to a sympathetic hearing of Falstaff's philosophy, which is diametrically opposed to everything the aristocrats proclaim. He must move us from one philosophy to another, from one mood to another, from one class to another, and still retain our sympathies for both. To accomplish this, he slides from the aristocrats by means of the duet of the prince and Falstaff to prepare smoothly for a sympathetic hearing of Falstaff. Hal is the only nobleman whose understanding and companionship with Falstaff can establish this bridge, and he introduces the subject of human fear, the only point that can validate Falstaff's catechism on honor. Without this transition we might view his soliloquy solely as comedy and miss the important truth it conveys.

Structure

Methods of Analyzing Structure

Structure and Art

The structure of art depends largely on its functions. Various functions have been proposed: entertainment, instruction, catharsis of unpleasant and unconstructive emotions, imitation and fantasy. Certain artistic structures obviously carry out these purposes. The "theme" or "point" of a work of art clearly expresses the function of instruction; the convention of the "hero," by encouraging audience identification, fulfils the "fantasy" function of art; and the "fourth wall" convention of modern theater was developed to intensify effective "imitation" in drama. Unfortunately, no two critics have ever agreed on all the functions of art, and viewing artistic structure purely in terms of function frequently complicates more than it simplifies. Nevertheless, while not consistently applicable in comprehending the structure of any given work of art, function gives invaluable clues to artistic structure and should be kept in mind in the analysis of any individual work.

Structure and Media

The structure of any work of art is obviously largely determined by the medium in which it appears. For instance, drama, cinema and music take place in time, as distinct from sculpture, art and architecture, which are spatial forms of art. As a result, music has developed the melody, which is a musical time structure, just as cinema and drama have made use of plot, which is a dramatic time structure. By the same token, the novel allows direct revelations of its characters' inner thoughts, which drama, a more realistic and direct imitation, cannot permit except by soliloquy, which is no longer allowed because of the greater realism of modern drama.

Considerations like these, of course, contribute largely to the structure and form of the various arts. To visualize the extent of the influence of media, one need only imagine how *Henry IV* might fare as a novel or a movie; obviously the structure and its final effect would be entirely different.

Structure as a Result of Contingencies

A work of art is dependent on the limitations of its creator, his level of culture, his audience and their level of culture, the comparative flexibility and the level of development of the art form in which he works. For instance, Shakespeare had just so many actors to work with in his company. He was aware of the limitations and excellences of each, and all of his dramas were created within the limits as they were thus defined. As an example, it is impossible to know how much of the figure of Falstaff we owe to Will Kempe, the clown of the Chamberlain's Men, and how much to pure invention on Shakespeare's part. Certainly Kempe was good at comedy and was a formidable ad-libber and already popular long before the organization of the Chamberlain's Men. Shakespeare gave him a comic part in most of the plays up to 1600 (when he left the group), not only because such buffoonery offered relief of dramatic tension (and all the other aesthetic critical reasons we moderns like to imagine), but also simply because his audiences looked forward to this kind of farce, whether it fitted in the play or not, and finally, just because Kempe was there to be used and there was no sense in wasting him. The actors were simply the givens with which Shakespeare had to work.

There are all sorts of similar chances, limitations and contingencies which can define the structure of drama, for it is the most communal of art forms, and hence the most susceptible to disruption. We are not so shocked today at the idea that a director might say to a playwright: "Will Baby, the fourth act's too short; whip up a little scene to tack on the end." We would not even be surprised if "Will Baby" was out with a cold and the producer knocked out a little scene that everybody else thought would pass. But we are outraged at the notion that such things might have happened with Shakespeare's plays, even though we know that these plays were written and produced at a white heat, ran for about ten performances, and were replaced by others in quick succession. The marvel is not that there are flaws, but that there is such incredible coherence and art in spite of all the contingencies which attended conception and performance.

Structure and Meaning

To a great extent, however, structure is not limited by the functions of art, the definition of medium and the hazards of contingency. It is established by the dramatist or author in an attempt to define and express the artistic material he wishes to communicate. In this sense, structure is directly related to the message or content of the play and furnishes the means whereby it can be expressed. This aspect of structure is the easiest and most rewarding for study and analysis because it directly expresses the will of the creator and gives the clearest clues to his intended meaning.

A series of pertinent questions will almost invariably open up this relationship between the form and the meaning of the work. "What are the problems presented in the beginning of the work?" "What is the author trying to say?" "Who is the hero?" "Who is the antagonist?" "What is the battle the hero must win?" "Does he win or lose?" "Why?" Such questions, if logically pursued, reveal that inner structure which reflects the inner vision of the creator.

Analysis of Structure

Henry IV, Part I was an early example of Shakespeare's mature development. Fortunately, he gained self-confidence before age had robbed his youthful genius of exuberance. The result is a play disarmingly simple at first appearance, yet enormously complex in structure and inner meaning. As proof of this, try to sum up what the play says in a paragraph. The task is impossible. The play "says" a thousand things, many of them almost impossible to put into words. Yet certain primary, broad structural meanings appear almost immediately, and after these are analyzed, others appear. By this method the various structures of the play can be gradually comprehended layer by layer, for on first reading or viewing, the structures pass unnoticed in the general impression of rich and vivid life enacted on the stage.

The Main Dramatic Plot

"Who is the hero of the play?" Prince Hal. "And who is his antagonist?" Harry Hotspur and the Percy family. "And over what stake do they fight?" Obviously, the crown. The essential, open conflict and the basic plot of the play then revolves around the rebellion, with Hal, the king, and the loyal nobles on one side, and the Percies, Douglas, Glendower, Mortimer and the Archbishop of York on the other.

This simple plot forms the backbone of the play. In the first scene Shakespeare introduces the king, and in the third, the Percies. By the end of the first act he has revealed the background of the conflict and brought the parties to an outright, official breach. During the second and third acts this primary plot is put on hold while the Falstaff plot is worked out. Only enough scenes of the rebellion are presented to remind us that complications are coming to a head. In Act IV the main plot is resumed and claims the stage right up to the end of the play. The outcome of the plot conflict is decided in the battle at Shrewsbury and is not fully revealed until the last scene of the play.

The Comic Subplot

The main plot is obviously not the only business of the play, and once we have analyzed and laid it aside, a secondary plot becomes obvious. It involves Prince Hal, Falstaff and their drinking companions in a robbery. The complications are introduced in the first act; the major action takes place in the second; and all its issues are fully resolved by the end of that act. But notice that this is a plot without a hero, an antagonist or even a clear-cut conflict. We might better describe it as an action in Aristotle's sense of the word, with a definite beginning (Act I, Sc. 2), a middle or climax (Act II, Sc. 2) and an end (Act II, Sc. 4). The central core of the action is, quite simply, the double robbery in which the bandits rob the travellers and Hal and Poins rob the bandits.

The connections between the main plot and this comic subplot are slight. There is a small overlapping of characters: Hal figures importantly in both plots, and Falstaff figures slightly in the end of the main plot. Otherwise, there is virtually no connection. The two plots have no effect on each other, and the symbolic similarity between the unlawful claiming of a crown and the robbery of a purse is flimsy. Therefore, Shakespeare must dance back and forth between plots trying to keep the play together.

The Musical Structure

But is all this moving back and forth merely to keep the various parties and plots in mind? This hypothesis is thrown in doubt by the appearance of Hal and the thieves in Act III, Sc. 3. The comic subplot has already been resolved, and there is no new or very important business in the scene. Why is it included?

It may be observed that Falstaff appears regularly all the way through the play, showing up every one or two scenes at least; he is never missing for more than two scenes in succession. If this scene in Act III were left out, he would be missing altogether for four scenes. Obviously, Shakespeare would not allow this, even though his appearance would make no significant contribution to either plot. The reason must be sought outside logical plot consideration.

It is to be found in the almost musical variation of moods in the play. Like a composer, Shakespeare is running two antithetical themes with contrasting variations and, in a very definite sense, the play is based on the contrast and harmony of their interplay. The first theme includes the formal, serious, eloquent world of the royal family and the noble rebels; the second includes the vulgar, humorous, zesty life of the thieves. Between the two themes is a contrast of mood, a difference of class and a disparity in the philosophical outlook on life. Shakespeare balances and harmonizes these differences for every bit of aesthetic contrast, sociological breadth, philosophical depth and emotional appeal they can add to the play.

The Symbolic Structure

After the main plot, the comic subplot and the contrasting musical structure of the play have been clarified, there remains a haunting sense that something is still uncomprehended. The most obvious source of this puzzlement is in the characters of Hotspur, Falstaff and the king. They seem to be saying more than the plot warrants, and there is a curious significance in their relation to Hal, whom they surround in a triangle of conflicting philosophies and life styles. To make any sense here, the critic must plunge from conscious and reasonable analysis into an obscure and shifting examination of symbolic meanings.

We have a hero surrounded by three thematic characters. First, consider the particular excellence of each. Falstaff steals from life, seeking its rewards without really paying for them. He is a robber and he is a player. Hotspur is a warrior, a killer. The king is a ruler. Robber, killer, ruler. Now is there any parallel in the hero's relation to the three of them? For instance, what is most significant in Hal's role with Hotspur? The answer is obvious: Hal kills the killer; he outdoes him at his own game. The principle holds true with the other characters. In the robbery at Gad's Hill Hal robs Falstaff, the robber himself. And in the final scenes of the play, by his exercise of responsibility and concern, he proves himself a better leader than his father. He outrules the ruler.

Furthermore, in each case there is a symbolic hint of a transfer of the peculiar excellence of thematic type to the hero. With Falstaff it is that illogical and seemingly unnecessary transfer of a cheap ring. With Hotspur it is the transfer of fame and glory. With the king it is a transfer of leadership.

Such is the symbolic structure. Certainly it is not immediately obvious in a first examination of the play. Yet so much of the satisfaction of its ending resides in the symbolic triumph of the hero, and that triumph was anticipated in the early challenges of the play. In the first scenes Hal was presented as a prince led astray by an old reprobate, a prince lacking both the military skill and the wisdom necessary to rule his nation. Before the play has ended, he has conquered all of these inferiorities, acquiring from those around him the necessary virtues.

Questions and Answers on Structure

Question 7.

There are actually only a few scenes of real physical action in the play, if we exclude exposition, argumentation, reaction and decision from our concept of action. List the scenes which contain important physical action and describe them briefly.

Answer

The robbery at Gad's Hill, where the money is stolen from the travellers and then restolen from the thieves by Poins and Hal, occurs in Act II, Sc. 2. Act V, Sc. 3 and 4, contain the battle at Shrewsbury, with an encounter between Douglas and Blunt, the king and Douglas, Hal and Douglas, Hal and Percy, and Falstaff and Douglas. Thus the essential action of the play resides in three scenes: the action of the comic subplot in one scene and the action of the main plot in two other scenes.

Question 8.

The meeting between the king and the prince in Act III, Sc. 2, contains the perfect elements for a minor dramatic climax. Describe those elements and explain how they are used.

Answer

By the time the scene begins, the audience has already been

prepared by the rehearsal in Act II, Sc. 4 for the issues which will now be settled. Will the king forgive his son? Will Hal honestly repent and change his ways? In brief, can father and son find a happy and constructive reconciliation?

In simple outline, the scene consists of an argument and scolding on the king's part, which calls forth a decision on Hal's. The first part of the scene (lines 1-159) is based on three passages of similar structure which are repeated in a rhythm of rising dramatic tension. Each passage begins with a criticism and is answered by the prince with an expression of repentance. But the effect of the king's three criticisms is cumulative. Going from an exposition of the prince's failings, he analyzes and compares them to Richard's follies, contrasts them unfavorably with his own, and finally culminates his emotional pressure on the prince by charging the son with being the father's worst enemy. Hal's responses increase in intensity until, at the final challenge, he breaks from mere repentance into a passionate vow to change his behavior and recover his lost reputation. At this climax of the whole scene Hal moves from reaction to that decision at which the king's argument has been directed, and once that decision is made, the tension of the scene diminishes rapidly.

With its mounting tension and rapid resolution, the scene serves well as a lesser climax, because it repeats, on the lower psychic level, the same build-up and release of tension so effective in the climax of physical action or battle. Here exposition leads to reaction, then to argument, and finally to decision. In physical action, argument leads to preparation and finally to physical combat and a final decision. The ratio of tensions is similar, but the increased violence, intensity and seriousness of actual battle make for a major climax, whereas the argument, which takes place on an intellectual level, is perfectly adapted for a minor climax.

Question 9.

List the functions of Act III, Sc. 3 in terms of various structures of the play.

Answer

In terms of the dramatic structure of the comic subplot, this scene is practically useless. It deals with the argument over the theft and value of Falstaff's ring, a rather trivial follow-up to the robbery at Gad's Hill. In terms of the symbolic plot, this scene reveals only that Hal fails to return the ring to Falstaff, a fact of only slight importance in the symbolic structure. However, in terms of the musical structure the scene is most important. It allows a return to low-life comedy between that very tense confrontation (Act III, Sc. 2) between the king and prince and the magnificent test of Hotspur's resolution in Act IV, Sc. 1.

Meaning

The Meaning of *Henry IV*, Part I

Exactly what *did* Shakespeare say in the play? To put it simply would require a modern writer about twice as many words as Shakespeare used himself. The reasons are obvious. First, Shakespeare was a master of compression and concentration; he could squeeze a maximum of meaning from a minimum of words. Second, many of his meanings are woven into the action of the play, and are never even verbalized. Thus, to put them in words would require another work of explanation, such as this. Finally, Shakespeare has presented in this play not one, but three rather complete philosophies of life; and the final statement is based not on a logical conclusion, but a synthesis of their contradictory claims. It is no easy matter to summarize his meaning in a sentence or two.

A History Play

Three types of drama were popular in Shakespeare's time: the comedy, the tragedy and the history. *Henry IV,* Part I is a "history play." The tragedy dealt with unhappy events and usually ended in a blood bath of murders and suicide. The comedy dealt with humor and romance in a lighter vein, and usually ended happily with the successful mating of lovers. The history play, popularized first by Marlowe, dealt of course with historical subjects, but it was a mixed genre, including tragic as well as comic elements, which combined well, so long as the dramatist followed the accepted outline of history with reasonable accuracy. If the writer was limited by historical facts, he was also freed from the proprieties of comedy and tragedy, which included rather fixed demands as to tone, subject and outcome. In other words, he could say things that were impossible to say in tragedy and comedy.

Henry IV, Part I gives evidence of this freedom. In presenting a rather short three-year period of English history, Shakespeare committed himself to the bare outlines of a rebellion whose main characters were fairly well known, and among them the irresponsible prince that later became one of England's great kings. Beyond this, Shakespeare was perfectly free to emphasize whatever elements he chose, introduce characters who pleased him, interpret others with almost limitless freedom, and establish whatever theme or slant seemed appropriate. He chose to concentrate on the development of the young prince — a subject neither tragic nor comic, but eminently serious — and he surrounded this central process with secondary elements, both comic (Falstaff) and tragic (Hotspur).

The Central Action

In dramatic tone, then, the play is mixed, but it is nevertheless unified in its focus on the rise in the fortunes of the prince, both in his victory over the rebellion and in his triumphant emergence as a superior man and leader. In other words, the play is based on a major development in the character and position of the prince, which may be defined as "the central action."

Now, few major actions of the world lead to simple conclusions. Any action is always more complex than all of the insights and conclusions we might bring to bear on it. The action itself is the essential material of drama, and the best we can do is turn on it the various lights of understanding, attempting to arrange the insights it provides into a coherent artistic arrangement.

Such is Shakespeare's approach in this play. There is no one meaning, but a multiplicity of them. He holds the action up to the understanding of his various characters, and from this he paints an impressionistic image of glittering contradiction. The result is a richness and depth of statement which defies pat analysis. In this play Shakespeare makes a thousand contradictory statements and, transcending them, makes one unique statement almost impossible to translate.

Nevertheless, it is important not only to classify the lesser statements of the play, but to attempt at least to articulate the greater statements as well. In this attempt we shall find it most helpful to divide Shakespeare's meaning into two general divisions: his statements about how things *are*, and those about how things *should* be.

The Political Statement

In his histories Shakespeare presented a general thesis that the assassination of Richard II and the usurpation of the crown by Henry IV created a social disruption which plagued England for several centuries, even through the War of the Roses. The apparent result of this continuing disruption was a self-perpetuating chain of injustices and revenges. For instance, Richard II wronged Bolingbroke by exiling him. Bolingbroke retaliated by deposing and murdering Richard. In *Henry IV*, Part I, to secure his position Bolingbroke (now Henry IV) wronged Mortimer, Richard's legal heir to the throne. To avenge Mortimer and pursue their own ambitions, the Percies joined in rebellion against Henry. Thus Shakespeare shows that violence against the legally established and traditionally honored forms of society leads to new injustices, and these in turn to others. In political philosophy this thesis is not unlike the Biblical moral hypothesis that "the sins of the father shall be visited on the son."

However, Shakespeare does not concentrate solely on external violence, which is after all but a symptom. He probes beneath the surface of political life to reveal the psychological mutilation created by the original disruption, and shows how it causes further unrest.

In *Henry IV*, Part I, he highlights the confusion of loyalties which inevitably resulted from the deposition of Richard. Even the Percies, who aided in the deposing of Richard, and of all men *should* have been loyal to Henry IV, find sudden regrets for their act and a new-found pity for the murdered Richard when it is to their advantage. Hotspur condemns his elders for their treachery:

> Shall it for shame be spoken in these days,
> Or fill up chronicles in time to come,
> That men of your nobility and power
> Did gage them both in an unjust behalf,
> (As both of you, God pardon it! have done)
> To put down Richard, that sweet lovely rose,
> And plant this thorn, this canker Bolingbroke?
>
> (Act I, Sc. 3, 170-176)

As a counterpart to disloyal subjects, Shakespeare presents a guilty, suspicious ruler. Henry guards his royal image with an almost obsessive jealousy and exhibits rage at the slightest mention of his debt to the Percies. His denial of the loyalty of Mortimer in the battle against Glendower is almost psychotic. Sensitive and vulnerable, he must dispose of Mortimer without daring to admit the reason, though every man in the kingdom knows it.

As in reflecting mirrors, the king's suspicion creates new disloyalty which in turn gives rise to new suspicions. Thus Worcester muses:

> And 'tis no little reason bids us speed,
> To save our heads by raising of a head;
> For, bear ourselves as even as we can,
> The King will always think him in our debt,
> And think we think ourselves unsatisfied,
> Till he hath found a time to pay us home.
>
> (Act I, Sc. 3, 280-285)

Thus, Shakespeare presents a social wound which every attempt at healing only serves to inflame. Most damaging of all, the usurpation sets an example of treachery and ambition which, as long as it succeeds, encourages others to imitation. Hotspur rants heatedly on the honor of Mortimer in Act I; Hotspur will crown him out of sheer vengeance against the king. Yet, as the play progresses, it becomes obvious that Mortimer's right is of little concern to the Percies and certainly of no concern to Worcester, who guides the family and manipulates Hotspur. It is no wild guess that Worcester, given victory at Shrewsbury, would seize the throne for himself and thereby follow the example set by Bolingbroke.

Yet usurpation and tyranny are but the symptoms of a tragic deficiency of political virtue. Once the legal sanctions of tradition are violated, the values of sound statecraft can easily be twisted to meet selfish demands, and the body politic itself becomes a prize of the dominion of power. Henry IV informs us of that fact in his response to Worcester's complaint:

> These things, indeed, you have articulate,
> Proclaimed at market crosses, read in churches,
> To face the garment of rebellion
> With some fine color that may please the eye
> Of fickle changelings and poor discontents,
> Which gape and rub the elbow at the news
> Of hurlyburly innovation.
> And never yet did insurrection want
> Such water colors to impaint his cause, . . .
>
> (Act V, Sc. 1, 72-80)

There is always an argument against the laws of the land, but once they are violated rather than changed by legal methods, a fatal wound has been created in the authority of the government which inevitably results in political instability. Such a wound may require many years to heal. This is Shakespeare's political thesis, and it bears up remarkably well in the light of European history. After its own internal revolutions, England required a hundred years or more to recover.

Shakespeare's Statements on the Generations of Man

In this play Shakespeare carefully marks the distinctions of age. Three ages are represented. Naïve youth with its horseplay and foolery, its animal appetites and robust vigor is represented by that overgrown child, Falstaff, and his companion Hal. Young manhood is represented by Hotspur with his self-disciplined devotion to heroism and duty, his idealism and his restless passion for life. The elders are blessed and plagued by that skeptical wisdom of age which accomplishes the most in this world and enjoys it the least.

In Shakespeare's vision each age has its own virtue and corresponding vice. Youth is self-indulgent and changeable. Manhood is driven by pride and passion. Age has solidified into selfish cynicism, forgetting the loves and joys of youth and incapable of the vision and energy of manhood. In brief, each age is insufficient in itself and requires completion through association with other ages. Thereby Shakespeare seems to say that a balanced and total approach to life can only be achieved by a consensus of the generations. Or, he hints at that improbable possibility — a man of such vitality that he could achieve each new stage of maturation, developing a balanced and competent personality flexibly adapted to all the requirements of life.

The Statement on the Social Classes

Henry IV covers a broad spectrum of economic and social classes, from kings to thieves. Shakespeare's depiction is inaccurate at times, subtly shaded for the purposes of dramatic contrast and aesthetic pleasure rather than a true depiction of reality. For instance, it is hard to believe that the lower classes were quite as lighthearted and carefree as they were depicted at his taverns and inns, or that the upper classes were so worn with care and deprived of innocent pleasures. Nevertheless, the play makes such regular distinctions, distorted though they may be.

The most notable artistic distinction is Shakespeare's use of blank verse for gentlemen and aristocrats, and prose for commoners. This linguistic variance symbolizes an underlying difference of spirit. The commoner's relaxation of grammatical structures reflects a relaxed attitude toward the rigid moral structures of society and a consequent spontaneity of behavior. The gentleman's carefully polished language speaks for his more self-conscious behavior determined by social standards which demand grace, virtue and dignity. For these strenuous achievements the gentleman must obviously sacrifice spontaneity.

The kings and the heads of the powerful aristocratic families reveal another standard of behavior which is almost as far removed from the standard of the gentleman as his is from the commoner's. Here spontaneity is not only set aside, but so is all play of emotion and self-expression as well, in a display of shrewd reasoning. As a result, the nobleman seems at times hardly more than a thinking machine, cunningly crafted to resemble a human being.

Breaches of the social code far outnumber adherence to it in this play. Falstaff's cronies present a panorama of lower-class vice, illustrating in the "ill-yoke humor" of their idleness, a lack of honesty, industry or loyalty to their masters and state. Rather than contributing to the society in which they exist, they prey upon it as parasites. And only by looking to minor figures, such as the carriers, Francis and Mistress Quickly, do we sense what is proper in the lower classes.

The same is true among the gentlemen. Westmoreland, Blunt and Vernon are perfect examples of behavior appropriate to an aristocrat. They are dignified, honest and exemplary in their loyalty to the lords they serve. But these are, after all, minor characters with minor virtues, dismally overwhelmed by the gross corruptions of Falstaff, who represents everything a gentleman should not be. He takes advantage of every right and betrays every responsibility of his position. He offers bad advice to the prince, leading him into idle pastimes; he uses his commission for personal gain, betraying his soldiers, ignoring his duty to his king and stealing the military honor of his prince and friend. For all his virtues and pleasures, Falstaff is a disgrace as a gentleman.

Prince Hal and Hotspur fare little better. Hal's behavior in the beginning of the play is only slightly better than Falstaff's, but far more outrageous considering his position as prince. The prince, as a future king, would be expected to sacrifice his own comforts (and certainly his whims and fancies) in the pursuit of royal virtues, but Hal reverses the process.

Hotspur, apparently better, has sacrificed his own pleasures and whims, but enslaved himself instead to an obsession for military glory and personal advancement. His wilful temperament distorts the dignity and sense of balance required of a noble. But primarily he fails in his social responsibility, throwing aside his obligations of loyalty to the king and the protection of his subordinates for personal grudges and harebrained adventures.

Of the great nobles, only Northumberland, Hotspur's father, reveals that selfless, reasoned exercise of concern and responsibility which should characterize the great and powerful. But his influence is smothered in the self-seeking conniving of Worcester and the reckless daring of Hotspur. Henry IV and Worcester are, unfortunately, two of a kind. One, a king, the other, leader of a great family and only slightly less than king, both play the game of power. Unfortunately this means power for selfish ends, not for the good of family or nation. All their self-discipline and experienced wisdom is perverted to petty and destructive ends.

The Types of Men and their Philosophies of Life

Shakespeare is speaking here of something more than generations and social classes. Fundamentally he is showing the various types of men and the fundamental attitudes toward life which make them different. It is an achievement to present in one play three such distinct types as Falstaff, Hotspur and the king, and present all of them so credibly in so intriguing a fashion. More than achievement, it is sheer genius to present the philosophy, the very rationale of existence, of all of them so winningly that, admitting them to be irreconcilable, it is impossible to choose one over the other. What sensitive person can deny the delight of Falstaff's gross obscenities or the wisdom of his catechism of honor? Who is rational enough to withstand Hotspur's fiery tribute to the bloody glories of war? And what person of sense can refute the cynical wisdom of Worcester and the king, who know the flaws of man and all the traps of experience?

Finally, it seems that here are not merely three types of men, but three parts of the mind of man, which will always argue over the conditions of existence and the pursuit of life. These are symbols of the elements of human nature which loom mysteriously about the figure of the prince — the central consciousness of the play — revealing in their partial incompleteness the virtues he must absorb, the petty contradictions he must transcend to achieve the full extension of the human possibility which resides in us all.

The Psychological Statement

A cursory glance at the play, however, reveals an interesting time sequence in Hal's incorporation of these three ways of thinking. First, he imitates and digests the attitudes of Falstaff; second, the prowess of Hotspur; and third, the leadership of the king. In a curious way this sequence of developments parallels the stages of psychic development from youth to manhood.

Falstaff represents the wild freedom and self-indulgence of childhood, which sees little beyond the pleasure of the moment. We might compare him to Huck Finn, that renegade from adult society, who stands on his own self-interest, viewing the dilemmas of adult life with disdain, skepticism and honesty. Yet it is the view of an uninvolved child who has answered none of the challenges and assumed none of the responsibilities of maturity, a child whose primary concern is his own comfort, his pleasures, his self-preservation.

Hotspur represents that later stage of youth — aspiring to, yet still falling short of complete manhood — which practises severe self-discipline in the pursuit of high ideals. It is that stage when boys excel at athletics, hunting, and other endeavors which develop self-discipline and endurance. It is a stage of active achievement, high idealism and quick impatience which overvalues will and underestimates any obstacles in the path of determination and perseverence.

The king represents a third stage of maturity, when the man realizes that all his ideals, self-discipline, and determination are worthless without a cold, realistic assessment of the potentialities and weaknesses of human nature. This is a phase of objective analysis, of hardheaded reason, of scientific endeavor.

These stages of psychic growth in the individual have been reflected in various theories and philosophies. They are roughly parallel to the various layers of psychic function theorized by Freud: the id, superego, and ego — the first representing instinct and primitive emotion, the second conscience and idealism, and the third reason and reality orientation.

But eventually, the prince achieves a fourth and final stage of maturation and a new excellence which all of the main characters have lacked: a sense of responsibility and a generous affection and loyalty to others. The illumination of his success casts a shadow of inadequacy on all that has occurred before. Falstaff, Hotspur, Worcester and the king — which of them has not failed in this respect?

The prince has achieved two singular victories by his final growth. He has attained all of the levels of maturity presented by the main characters, without sacrificing any of the others, thus uniting the realism of the king with the heroic spirit of Hotspur and the joyous spontaneity of Falstaff.

Second, he has passed on to another level achieved by none of the others — a true recognition of the social inter-dependence of man. He alone has discovered that no man is self-sufficient, that the laws of social interaction cannot be violated or dismissed without penalty, that, far from granting exemption, the exercise of power demands an increase of responsibility. Thus, he achieves a double victory of surpassing maturity.

The Perfect Man

In terms of each of the play's statements, the prince as he appears in the final scenes offers the resolving force, the unifying factor, the culminating virtue. He has overcome the vices of his youth. He has proved his value to England, and thus won the loyalty of his subjects and established his right to be king. He has fulfilled the needs and expectations of his social role: he plays the part of a king perfectly. Finally, he has imitated and surpassed all the virtues of the play and the men in whom they were represented. All the lines of Shakespeare's meaning cross in the completed figure of Hal, who blends all contradictions into one final unity, the perfect man and prince.

Questions and Answers on Meaning

Question 10.

Falstaff helps to establish and define the values of the play. Mention some of these values and the way in which he reaffirms them.

Answer

Near the beginning of the play, where no serious issues are at stake, Falstaff's cowardice at Gad's Hill is hilariously funny. In battle, however, where the fate of his army, prince, king, and even his nation is at stake, his cowardice appears nothing less than contemptible, and the audience which had smiled tolerantly at his rationalizations, pitied his honest expressions of fear and sympathized with his philosophy of self-preservation now suddenly sees the ugly consequences of his cowardice and is forced to reject it.

Falstaff delights in betraying the proprieties of existence. Where modesty is required, he boasts; for honesty, he substitutes lies; for sense he substitutes nonsense. And this overturning of accepted values and expectations is pleasantly shocking and humorous in the early acts of the play. But when in battle he offers the prince a bottle of sack instead of a pistol, his humor has worn terribly thin. The audience is forced to recognize that there is a time for all things, that there are reasons for proprieties, and disastrous consequences can result from their casual dismissal.

Falstaff and his cronies delight in down-playing the loyalty and faith men are supposed to extend one another. The old man curses the prince behind his back; he misrepresents the facts of the robbery; and Poins and Hal delight in betraying their friends. But disloyalty is thrown into an entirely new light when Falstaff weakens his battle company to line his own pockets, shirks his duties, and finally steals Hal's claim to having killed Hotspur. Then disloyalty appears in its true light: a betrayal of faith and trust.

It is clear that, by presenting such vices as these, Falstaff challenges and frequently shatters superficial standards of society. But later, by stretching these same humorous vices to outrageous betrayals, he forces the audience to recognize the nucleus of truth which established the social values in the first place.

Question 11.

How does the character of Prince Hal fail to support the meaning of the play?

Answer

Although all of the solutions of the play are worked out through development of the prince, he is never quite convincing as a real human being. By the end of the play one must agree that he is brave, generous, honest, loyal and responsible, but unfortunately these virtues do not create dramatic credibility for his character.

A cliché is unfortunately applicable here: Prince Hal is too good to be true. First, it is hard to believe that such a model of virtue ever existed. Second, Shakespeare has so cleared his behavior of faults that nothing remains of those eccentricities and excesses which add so much to the credibility of dramatic characterization. One feels that Hal might come alive if he had a tic, or drank to excess, or did almost anything to shatter that bland virtue which is too perfect in the last scenes.

While we recognize the prince as a virtuous hero, we are far more impressed with the lovable follies of Falstaff and the misguided heroics of Hotspur. We remember the erring, impartial characters long after we have forgotten Hal, the keystone of the whole structure, and this division of attention detracts from the meaning of the play.

Question 12.

How do the major characters, in words and actions, comment on the theme of honor and death?

Answer

Of all the major characters, Falstaff makes the most unique and oft-remarked comment on honor and death. In time of danger, which he avoids if he can, he behaves like a coward. He runs from one duel at Gad's Hill, and in the battle of Shrewsbury he pretends to be dead to get out of another. The old man is perfectly honest with himself about his cowardice and his preference of life over honorable death, and his conviction furnishes the basis of his famous soliloquy. However, he maintains a semblance of courage, and he presents a fictitious image of his own bravery where possible to the eyes of the world.

Hotspur's behavior, both his words and his actions, coincides with the official values of honor and courage professed by society. He is utterly fearless, doubting neither his own supremacy in battle nor the hazards which might weaken it. To this extent he is both admirable and foolish. He is, however, true to his philosophy even as he faces death. Defeated by the prince, he regrets loss of honor more than loss of life.

The king does not speak at all of honor and death, but his actions reflect his attitudes. Probably he is not deeply concerned with death since his life is almost completed. He is even less concerned with the shows of honor because he values too highly the inner substance of power. For that power he will take risks, but no more than necessary. He wisely sends other nobles into battle dressed in armor to confuse the enemy and draw danger from himself. The king does little for honor, but he will evade *dishonor* at any cost. Notice that in his battle disguise, he still wears his own armor to avoid accusations of cowardice, and when challenged by Douglas, he will not flee, even though he is badly outclassed.

The statement of Prince Hal on the subject of honor and death is perhaps more subtle and complex than any other. He is obviously afraid neither of battle nor death. His words to Falstaff proclaim it in Act II, Sc. 4. More important, his behavior in battle against both Douglas and Hotspur, the most formidable of his enemies, proves it.

Yet the subtlety of his position lies not in his courage but in his motives for it. Hal seeks honor not as an end in itself. He does not care for that romantic ideal of glory and honor which inspires Hotspur and somehow justifies, for Hotspur at least, his early death. Hal seeks honor as a necessary complement of royal reputation, knowing that he must defeat Hotspur to establish his own supremacy as the first man in the land. For this great prize, which is rightfully his, he will risk his life.

Selected Criticisms

Perhaps no authour has ever in two plays [the two parts of *Henry IV*] afforded so much delight. The great events are interesting, for the fate of kingdoms depend upon them; the slighter occurrences are diverting, and, except one or two, sufficiently probable; the incidents are multiplied with wonderful fertility of invention, and the characters diversified with the utmost nicety of discernment, and the profoundest skill in the nature of man. The prince . . . is a young man of great abilities and violent passions, whose sentiments are right, though his actions are wrong; whose virtues are obscured by negligence, and whose understanding is dissipated by levity . . . This character is great, original, and just . . . But *Falstaff* unimitated, unimitable *Falstaff,* how shall I describe thee? Thou compound of sense and vice; of sense which may be admired but not esteemed, of vice which may be despised, but hardly detested. *Falstaff* is a character loaded with faults, and with those faults which naturally produce contempt. He is a thief, and a glutton, a coward, and a boaster, always ready to cheat the weak, and prey upon the poor; to terrify the timorous and insult the defenceless. At once obsequious and malignant, he satirizes in their absence those on whom he lives by flattering. He is familiar with the prince only as an agent of vice, but of this familiarity he is so proud as not only to be supercilious and haughty with common men, but to think his interest of importance to the duke of *Lancaster.* Yet the man thus corrupt, thus despicable, makes himself necessary to the prince that despises him, by the most pleasing of all qualities, perpetual gaiety, by an unfailing power of exciting laughter, which is the more freely indulged, as his wit is not of the splendid or ambitious kind, but consists in easy escapes and sallies of levity, which make sport but raise no envy. It must be observed that he is stained with no enormous or sanguinary crimes, so that his licentiousness is not so offensive but that it may be borne for his mirth. The moral to be drawn from this representation is, that no man is more dangerous than he that with a will to corrupt hath the power to please; and that neither wit nor honesty ought to think themselves safe with such a companion when they see Henry seduced by Falstaff.

Samuel Johnson

The ideas which I have formed concerning the Courage and Military Character of the Dramatic Sir *John Falstaff,* are so different from those which I find generally to prevail in the world, that I shall take the liberty of stating my sentiments on the subject . . . I do not clearly discern that Sir *John Falstaff* deserves to bear the character so generally given him of an absolute Coward; . . . I do not conceive *Shakespeare* ever meant to make Cowardice an essential part of his constitution . . . I know how universally the contrary opinion prevails . . .

We see this extraordinary Character, almost in the first moment of our acquaintance with him, involved in circumstances of apparent dishonour; and we hear him familiarly called *Coward* by his most intimate companions. We see him, on occasion of the robbery at *Gads-Hill,* in the very act of running away from the Prince and *Poins;* and we behold him, on another of more honourable obligation, in open day light, in battle, and acting in his profession as a Soldier, escaping from *Douglas* even out of the world as it were; and we find him on the former occasion, betrayed into those *lies* and *braggadocioes,* which are the usual concomitants of Cowardice in Military men, and pretenders to valour . . .

We all like *Old Jack;* yet, by some strange perverse fate, we all abuse him, and deny him the possession of any one single good or responsible quality. There is something extraordinary in this: It must be a strange art in *Shakespeare* which can draw our liking and good will towards so offensive an object. He has wit, it will be said; cheerfulness and humour of the most characteristic and captivating sort. And is this enough? Is the humour and gaiety of vice so very captivating? . . . Or does not the apparency of such humour, and the flashes of such wit, by more strongly disclosing the deformity of character, but the more effectually excite our hatred and contempt of the man? And yet this is not our *feeling* of Falstaff's character . . .

It may not perhaps be easy . . . to resolve how it comes about, that, whilst we look upon *Falstaff* as a character of the like nature with that of *Parolles* or of *Bobadil,* we should preserve for him a great deal of respect and good-will, and yet feel the highest disdain and contempt of the others, tho' they are all involved in similar situations . . . Perhaps, after all, the *real* character of *Falstaff* may be different from his *apparent* one; and possibly this difference between reality and appearance, whilst it accounts at once for our liking and our censure, may be the point of humour in the character, and the source of all our laughter and delight . . .

To me then it appears that the leading quality in *Falstaff's* character . . . is a high degree of wit and humour, accompanied with great natural vigour and alacrity of mind. This quality so accompanied, led him probably very early into life, and made him highly acceptable to society; so acceptable,as to make it seem unnecessary for him to acquire any other virtue. Hence, perhaps, his continued debaucheries and dissipations of every kind. — He seems, by nature, to have had a mind free of malice or any evil principle; but he never took the trouble of acquiring any good one. He found himself esteemed and beloved with all his faults; nay *for* his faults, which were all connected with humour, and for the most part, grew out of it . . . He appeared more dissolute thro' ostentation. To the character of wit and humour, . . . he appears to have added a very necessary support, *that* of the profession of a *Soldier.* He had from nature, as I presume to say, a spirit of boldness and enterprise; which in a Military age . . . kept him always among the Great, and suited best both with his particular mode of humour and of vice. Thus living continually in society, nay even in Taverns, and indulging himself, and being indulged by others, in every debauchery; drinking, whoring, gluttony, and ease; assuming a liberty of fiction, necessary perhaps to his wit, and often falling into falsity and lies, he seems to have set, by degrees, all sober reputation at defiance; and finding eternal resources in his wit, he borrows, shifts, defrauds, and even robs, without dishonour. — Laughter and approbation attend his greatest excesses; and being governed visibly by no settled bad principle or ill design, fun and humour account for and cover all. By degrees, . . . he acquires bad habits, becomes an humourist, grows enormously corpulent, and falls into the infirmities of age; yet never quits, all the time, one single levity or vice of youth, or loses any of that chearfulness of mind, which had enabled him to pass thro' this course with ease to himself and delight to others; and thus, at last mixing youth and age, enterprize and corpulency, wit and folly, poverty and expence, title and buffoonery, innocence as to purpose, and wickedness as to practice; neither incurring hatred by bad principle, or contempt by Cowardice, yet involved in circumstances productive of imputation in both; a butt and a wit, a humourist and a man of humour, a touchstone and a laughing stock, a jester and a jest, has Sir *John Falstaff,* taken at that period of his life in which we see him, become the most perfect Comic character that perhaps ever existed . . .

Maurice Morgann

In order that a drama may be properly historical, it is necessary that it should be the history of the people to whom it is addressed. In the composition, care must be taken that there appear no dramatic improbability, as the reality is taken for granted. It must, likewise, be poetical; that only, I mean, must be taken which is the permanent in our nature, which is common, and therefore deeply interesting to all ages. The events themselves are immaterial, otherwise than as the clothing and manifestation of the spirit that is working within. In this mode, the unity resulting from succession is destroyed, but is supplied by a unity of a higher order, which connects the events by reference to the workers, gives a reason for them in the motives, and presents men in their causative character. It takes, therefore, that part of real history which is the least known, and infuses a principle of life and organization into the naked facts, and makes them all the framework of the animated whole . . .

The history of our ancient kings — the events of their reigns, I mean, — are like stars in the sky; — whatever the real interspaces may be, and however great, they seem close to each other. The stars — the events — strike us and remain in our eye, little modified by the difference of dates. An historic drama is, therefore, a collection of events borrowed from history, but connected together in respect of cause and time, poetically and by dramatic fiction . . .

In this, the first introduction of Falstaff [Act I, Sc. 2] observe the consciousness and the intentionality of his wit, so that when it does not flow of its own accord, its absence is felt, and an effort visibly made to recall it. Note also how Falstaff's pride is gratified in the power of influencing a prince of the blood, the heir apparent, by means of it. Hence his dislike to Prince John of Lancaster, and his mortification when he finds his wit fail on him.

Samuel Taylor Coleridge

If Shakespeare's fondness for the ludicrous sometimes led to faults in his tragedies (which was not often the case) he has made us amends by the character of Falstaff. This is perhaps the most substantial comic character that ever was invented. Sir John carries a most portly presence in the mind's eye; and in him, not to speak it profanely, 'we behold the fulness of the spirit of wit and humour bodily.' We are as well acquainted with his person as his mind, and his jokes come upon us with double force and relish from the quantity of flesh through which they make their way, as he shakes his fat sides with laughter, or "lards the lean earth as he walks along." Other comic characters seem, if we approach and handle them, to resolve themselves into air, 'into thin air'; but this is embodied and palpable to the grossest apprehension: it lies 'three fingers deep upon the ribs,' it plays about the lungs and the diaphragm with all the force of animal enjoyment. His body is like a good estate to his mind, from which he receives rents and revenues of profit and pleasure in kind, according to its extent, and the richness of the soil. Wit is often a meagre substitute for pleasurable sensation; an effusion of spleen and petty spite at the comforts of others, from feeling none in itself. Falstaff's wit is an emanation of a fine constitution; an exuberance of good-humour and good-nature; an overflowing of his love of laughter and good-fellowship; a giving vent to his heart's ease, and over-contentment with himself and others. He would not be in character, if he were not so fat as he is; for there is the greatest keeping in the boundless luxury of his imagination and the pampered self-indulgence of his physical appetites. He manures and nourishes his mind with jests, as he does his body with sack and sugar. He carves out his jokes, as he would a capon or a haunch of venison, where there is *cut and come again;* and pours out upon them the oil of gladness. His tongue drops fatness, and in the chambers of his brain 'it snows of meat and drink.' He keeps up perpetual holiday and open house, and we live with him in a round of invitations to a rump and dozen. — Yet we are not to suppose that he was a mere sensualist. All this is as much in imagination as in reality. His sensuality does not engross and stupify his other faculties, but 'ascends me into the brain, clears away all the dull, crude vapours that environ it, and makes it full of nimble, fiery, and delectable shapes.' His imagination keeps up the ball after his senses have done with it. He seems to have even a greater enjoyment of the freedom from restraint, of good cheer, of his ease, of his vanity, in the ideal exaggerated description which he gives of them, than in fact. He never fails to enrich his discourse with allusions to eating and drinking, but we never see him at table. . . . His pulling out the bottle in the field of battle is a joke to shew his contempt for glory accompanied with danger. . . . Again, such is his deliberate exaggeration of his own vices, that it does not seem quite certain whether the account of his hostess's bill, found in his pocket, with such an out-of-the-way charge for capons and sack with only one halfpenny-worth of bread, was not put there by himself as a trick to humour the jest upon his favourite propensities, and as a conscious caricature of himself. He is represented as a liar, a braggart, a coward, a glutton, etc., and yet we are not offended but delighted with him; for he is all these as much to amuse others as to gratify himself. . . .

The secret of Falstaff's wit is for the most part a masterly presence of mind, an absolute self-possession, which nothing can disturb. His repartees are involuntary suggestions of his self-love; instinctive evasions of everything that threatens to interrupt the career of his triumphant jollity and self-complacency. His very size floats him out of all his difficulties in a sea of rich conceits; and he turns around on the pivot of his convenience, with every occasion and at a moment's warning. . . .

The heroic and serious part of these two plays founded on the story of Henry IV is not inferior to the comic and farcical. The characters of Hotspur and Prince Henry are two of the most beautiful and dramatic, both in themselves and from contrast, that ever were drawn. They are the essence of chivalry. We like Hotspur the best upon the whole, perhaps because he was unfortunate. — The characters of their fathers, Henry IV and old Northumberland, are kept equally well. Henry naturally succeeds by his prudence and caution in keeping what he has got; Northumberland fails in his enterprise from an excess of the same quality, and is caught in the web of his own cold, dilatory policy. Owen Glendower is a masterly character. It is as bold and original as it is intelligible and thoroughly natural. The disputes between him and Hotspur are managed with infinite address and insight into nature. . . .

The peculiarity and excellence of Shakespeare's poetry is, that it seems as if he made his imagination the hand-maid of nature, and nature the plaything of his imagination. He appears to have been all the characters, and in all the situations he describes. It is as if either he had

had all their feelings, or had lent them all his genius to express themselves. There cannot be stronger instances of this than Hotspur's rage when Henry IV forbids him to speak of Mortimer, his insensibility to all that his father and uncle urge to calm him, and his fine abstracted apostrophe to honour, 'By heaven, methinks it were an easy leap,' etc. After all, notwithstanding the gallantry, generosity, good temper, and idle freaks of the mad-cap Prince of Wales, we should not have been sorry if Northumberland's force had come up in time to decide the fate of the battle at Shrewsbury; at least, we always heartily sympathize with Lady Percy's grief [*Henry IV,* Part II].

William Hazlitt.

Both parts of *Henry IV* consist of a comedy and a history fused together. The hero of the one is the royal Bolingbroke, the hero of the other is Falstaff, while Prince Henry passes to and fro between the history and the comedy, serving as the bond which unites the two. Both first and second parts, but especially the first part, were written with the utmost spirit and energy. Henry IV is the same Bolingbroke who had been so greatly conceived in *King Richard II;* only he is no longer in the full force of his manhood. He is worn by care and toil, harassed by the troubles of the unquiet times, yet still resolved to hold firmly what he has forcibly attained. He has tried flattery with his turbulent nobles, and he has tried to overawe them; but still they are not made loyal subjects. Scotland, Wales, the lords of the North, are in arms against him. There is a pathetic power in the figure of this weary, ambitious man, who can take no rest until the rest of death comes to him.

Hotspur, who to bring him into contrast with the Prince, is made much younger than the Harry Percy of history, is as ardent in the pursuit of glory as the Prince seems to be indifferent to it. To his hot temper, and quick sense of personal honour, small matters are great; he does not see things in their true proportions; he lacks self-control, he has no easiness of nature. Yet he is gallant chivalrous, not devoid of generosity nor of quick affections, though never in a high sense disinterested. The Prince, whom Shakespeare admires and loves more than any other person in English history, afterwards to become Shakespeare's ideal king of England, cares little for mere reputation. He does not think much of himself, and of his own honour; and while there is nothing to do, and his great father holds all power in his own right hand, Prince Hal escapes from the cold proprieties of the court to the boisterous life and mirth of the tavern. He is, however, only waiting for a call to action, and Shakespeare declares that from the first he was conscious of his great destiny, and while seeming to scatter his force in frivolity, was holding his true self, well guarded, in reserve. . . .

Falstaff is everything in little, or rather everything in *much;* for, is he not a tun of flesh? English literature knows no humourous creation to set beside Falstaff; and to find his equal — yet his opposite — we must turn to the gaunt figure of the romantic knight of La Mancha, in whose person Cervantes smiles away pathetically the chivalry of the Middle Ages from out our modern world. Falstaff exercises upon the reader of these plays much the same fascination which he exercised upon the Prince. We know him to be a gross-bodied, self-indulgent old sinner, devoid of moral sense and of self-respect, and yet we cannot part with him. We cannot live in this mixed world without humour, and Falstaff is humour maintaining its mastery against all antagonisms.

Edward Dowden

Up to a certain point Falstaff is ludicrous in the same way as many other figures, his distinction being in the mere abundance of ludicrous traits. Why should we laugh at an old man with a huge belly and corresponding appetites; at the inconveniences he suffers on a hot day, or in playing the footpad, or when he falls down and there are no levers to lift him? . . . But these things do not explain why besides laughing at Falstaff, we are made happy by him and laugh *with* him. . . .

The main reason why he makes us happy and puts us so entirely at our ease is that he himself is happy and entirely at ease. 'Happy' is too weak a word; he is in bliss, and we share his glory. . . . His ease and enjoyment are not simply those of the happy man of appetite; they are those of the humorist of genius. Instead of being comic to you and serious to himself, he is more ludicrous to himself than to you; and he makes himself out more ludicrous than he is, in order that he and others may laugh. . . .

No one in the play understands Falstaff fully. . . . Poins and the prince delight in him; they get him into corners for the pleasure of seeing him escape in ways they cannot imagine; but they often take him much too seriously. Poins rarely sees, the prince does not alway see, and moralizing critics never see, that when Falstaff speaks ill of a companion behind his back . . . he knows quite well what he says will be repeated, . . . being certain that it can only give him an opportunity for humour. It is the same with his lying. . . .

The main source of our sympathetic delight in Falstaff is his humourous superiority to everything serious, and the freedom of soul enjoyed in it.

A. C. Bradley

To poise character against character was an element in Shakespeare's art . . . and so, having made the vessel of porcelain, Richard II, he had to make the vessel of clay, Henry V. He makes him the reverse of Richard. He has the gross vices, the coarse nerves, of one who is to rule among violent people, and he is so little 'too friendly' with his friends that he bundles them out of doors when their time is over [at the end of *Henry IV,* Part II]. He is as remorseless and undistinguished as some natural force.

William Butler Yeats

The King, though the titular hero, is not a dramatic centre of the play. He claims precedence, however, as the main link with *Richard II*. . . . Under the royal robe and crown we see the figure of the old Bolingbroke, in all essentials unchanged. . . . Diplomacy and determination enabled him to wrest the crown from Richard's feeble hands, and they enable him to keep it firmly in his grasp. But they cannot make him successful in the highest sense, either as a man or as a king; and they cannot, above all, yield him the inward peace for which he sighs . . . . As he confesses on his death-bed, it was by 'by-paths and indirect crook'd ways' that he 'met' his crown, only to find it sit troublesome upon his head. Richard's prophecies of woe to come are fulfilled. The shrewd, self-reliant politician cannot blossom into a benignant sovereign, loving and beloved. With all his talents and virtues, he lacks the integrity of nature and the personal magnetism which rivet permanently the attachment of men. The opening scene shows him already at fault both as a father and a king. . . . Thus he completely misunderstands his eldest son, and we hear him lamenting that unkind fate has given him as heir his young Harry instead of Hotspur. But, in spite of this, he treats Hotspur with almost equal lack of insight. To him and to his father, Northumberland, Henry had in great measure owed his crown. Nor have their services ended there. The play opens with the account of Hotspur's victory over a formidable Scotch invading force, headed by the valiant Douglas. Henry has every motive to treat the Percys, and expecially this gallant scion of the house, with whole-hearted trust and gratitude. But he is a prey to the fear that those who have set him up in place of their lawful lord may at any moment turn against the ruler of their own making. Hence he seizes on what seems a favourable opportunity for humbling their pretension. . . . Henry's own conduct stirs up the formidable rebellion which unites against him the Percys, the Archbishop of York, the Welsh under Glendower, . . . and the Scots headed by Douglas, whom Hotspur has converted from friend to foe. But if the king is to blame that the rising should take place at all, he displays in coping with it all his former skill and resolution . . . He fights bravely amidst his troops, though with characteristic 'policy' he sends into the field a number of counterfeit kings. The battle won, he shows clemency to all but the chief offenders. . . .

Throughout the political convulsion he [King Henry] has been haunted by the bitter thought of his eldest son's misdoings, which his irritable conscience interprets as the retribution upon his own sins. And what rankles most is the apparent similarity of Prince Henry's conduct to that of Richard, while in Hotspur he sees the image of his younger self. . . . Not honour, but self-interest has been his guiding principle, yet the interest of the sagacious statesman has coincided at many points with that of his country. The usurper has been in no way a tyrant, yet his heart has been lacerated by not a few of those unseen stripes and scars which . . . are the tyrant's portion. For it is one of Shakespeare's great though unobtrusive triumphs to have shown in Bolingbroke's career that material success, exclusively pursued, turns to bitterness even in the hands of those best equipped to achieve it.

Frederick S. Boas

Over against Richard II it was Shakespeare's plan to set, not the crafty and reserved Bolingbroke, but his son, Henry V, the darling of the people, a lusty hero, open of heart and hand, unthrifty and dissolute in youth, in riper age the support and glory of the nation. . . . Yet Henry V is not so inwardly conceived as Richard II. His qualities are more popular and commonplace. Shakespeare plainly admires him, and feels toward him none of that resentment which the spectacle of robust energy and easy success produces in weaker tempers. If Henry, as Prince and King, falls short in some respects of the well-knit perfection that was intended, it is the price which he pays for admitting into his companionship a greater than himself, who robs him of his virtue and makes him a satellite in a larger orbit. Less tragic than Richard, less comic than Falstaff, the poor prince is hampered on both sides. . . .

Falstaff is a comic Hamlet, stronger in practical resource, and hardly less rich in thought. He is in love with life as Hamlet is out of love with it; he cheats and lies with no hesitation and no afterthought; he runs away or counterfeits death with more courage than others show in deeds of daring. The accidents and escapades of his life give ever renewed occasion for the triumph of spirit over matter, and show us the real man, above them all and aloof from them, calm, aristocratic, fanciful, scorning opinion, following his own ends, and intellectual to his finger-tips.

Sir Walter Raleigh

The King . . . is a swollen, soured, bullying man, with all the ingratitude of a king and all the baseness of one who knows his cause to be wrong. . . .

Prince Henry is not a hero, he is not a thinker, he is not even a friend; he is a common man whose incapacity for feeling enables him to change his habits whenever interest bids him.

John Masefield

In the portrayal of Falstaff the moods of comedy and farce are curiously interwoven. The comic spirit is busiest with him when he is aroused to an uneasy consciousness that his earthy mode of life requires some justification. . . . His quick wits are always ready to save him from some dire humiliation, to the brink of which he has been led by his cowardice or greed.

E. K. Chambers

Hotspur is testy and splenetic and impatient of pretence, as are the characters in later English novels; and Henry V, how English he is — so practical, sportsmanlike, moral, and pious; so manly and stalwart, and yet free and easy; so serious, and yet simple and humorous.

E. E. Stoll

As a man, he [Henry IV] is unattractive, cold, secretive. He can suppress or hide every tremor of personal sentiment and natural instinct . . . . He is set over against Hotspur, who, as a man, has the irresistible attractiveness of high-spirited nobility . . . but because Hotspur is so much at the mercy of his human and manly instincts, he is a complete political failure. He cannot govern because he cannot control and organize even himself.

H. B. Charlton

No play of Shakespeare's is better . . . Nothing that he wrote is more crowded with life or happier in its imitation of human talk. The pen that moves across these pages is perfectly free of itself. The host of persons assembled for our pleasure can say anything for their author he wants to say. The poetry of Hotspur and the prose of Falstaff have never been surpassed in their respective categories; the History as a dramatic form ripens here to a point past which no further growth is possible.

Mark Van Doren

Bibliography

Auden, W. H. "The Fallen City: Some Reflections on Shakespeare's 'Henry IV'," *Encounter,* XIII: 5, 1959, pp. 21-31.

Barber, C. L. *Shakespeare's Festive Comedy.* Princeton: Princeton University Press, 1959.

Berkeley, David, and Eidson, Donald. "The Theme of *Henry IV,* Part 1," *Shakespeare Quarterly,* XIX, 1968, pp. 25-31.

Campbell, Lily Bess. *Shakespeare's "Histories," Mirrors of Elizabethan Policy.* San Marino, California: The Huntington Library, 1947.

Charlton, H. B. *Shakespearian Comedy.* London: Methuen, 1938.

Empson, William. "Falstaff and Mr. Dover Wilson." *Kenyon Review,* XV, 1953, pp. 213-262.

Hapgood, Robert. "Falstaff's Vocation," *Shakespeare Quarterly,* XVI, 1965, pp. 91-98.

Hemingway, Samuel B. "On Behalf of That Falstaff," *Shakespeare Quarterly,* III, 1952, pp. 307-311.

Jenkins, Harold. *The Structural Problem in Shakespeare's Henry the Fourth.* London: Methuen, 1956.

Kaiser, Walter. *Praisers of Folly.* Cambridge: Harvard University Press, 1963.

Kris, Ernst. "Prince Hal's Conflict," *Psychoanalytic Quarterly,* XVII, 1948, pp. 487-506.

Levin, Lawrence L. "Hotspur, Falstaff and the Emblem of Wrath in *1 Henry IV,*" *Shakespeare Studies*, X, 1977, pp. 43-66.

McGuire, Richard L. "The Play-within-the-Play in *1 Henry IV.*" *Shakespeare Quarterly,* XVIII, 1967, pp. 47-52.

McNeir, Waldo. "Structure and Theme in the First Tavern Scene of Henry IV, Part One," *Essays on Shakespeare,* ed. G. R. Smith, pp. 67-83. University Park: Pennsylvania State University Press, 1965.

Muir, Kenneth. *The Sources of Shakespeare's Plays.* New Haven: Yale University Press, 1978.

Reese, M. M. *The Cease of Majesty.* New York: St. Martin's Press, 1961.

Richmond, H. M. *Shakespeare's Political Plays.* New York: Random House, 1967.

Shaw, John. "The Staging of Parody and Parallels in *1 Henry IV.*" *Shakespeare Survey,* XX, 1967, pp. 61-73.

Sjoberg, Elsa. "From Madcap Prince to King," *Shakespeare Quarterly, XX, 1969, pp. 11-16.*

Sorrelius, Gunnar. "The Smock Alley Prompt-Books of *1* and *2 Henry IV,*" *Shakespeare Quarterly,* XXII, 1971, pp. 111-128.

Spivack, Bernard. "Falstaff and the Psychomachia," *Shakespeare Quarterly,* VIII, 1957, pp. 449-459.

Sprague, Arthur Colby. "Gadshill Revisited," *Shakespeare Quarterly,* IV, 1953, pp. 125-137.

Stewart, J. I. M. *Character and Motive in Shakespeare.* London: Longman's, Green, 1949.

Stoll, E.E. *Shakespeare Studies.* New York: Macmillan, 1927.

Tillyard, E. M. W. *Shakespeare's History Plays.* New York: Macmillan, 1946.

Toliver, Harold E. "Falstaff, the Prince, and the History Play," *Shakespeare Quarterly,* XVI, 1965, pp. 63-80.

Traversi, D. A. *Shakespeare from Richard II to Henry V.* Stanford: Stanford University Press, 1957.

Wilson, J. Dover. *The Fortunes of Falstaff.* New York: MacMillan, 1944.

NOTES

NOTES